THE SUITCASE IN THE ATTIC

Daphne Neville

Copyright © 2018 Daphne Neville

All rights reserved, including the right to reproduce this book, or portions thereof in any form. No part of this text may be reproduced, transmitted, downloaded, decompiled, reverse engineered, or stored, in any form or introduced into any information storage and retrieval system, in any form or by any means, whether electronic or mechanical without the express written permission of the author.

This is a work of fiction. Names and characters are the product of the author's imagination and any resemblance to actual persons, living or dead, is entirely coincidental.

The views expressed in this work are solely those of the author and do not necessarily reflect the views of the publisher, and the publisher hereby disclaims any responsibility for them.

ISBN: 978-0-244-97785-6

PublishNation, London
www.publishnation.co.uk

Other Titles by This Author

TRENGILLION CORNISH MYSTERY SERIES
The Ringing Bells Inn
Polquillick
Sea, Sun, Cads and Scallywags
Grave Allegations
The Old Vicarage
A Celestial Affair
Trengillion's Jubilee Jamboree

PENTRILLICK CORNISH MYSTERY SERIES
The Chocolate Box Holiday
A Pasty In A Pear Tree

The Old Tile House

Chapter One

2017

High up in the cloudless blue sky, a solitary buzzard drifted on a current of warm air keeping a watchful eye out for prey in the fields below. It paid no attention to the purple train which twisted and turned through the Cornish landscape, past a woodland and beneath a bridge where it came out alongside a stretch of golden sand and the sea which sparkled in the afternoon sunshine.

Zac Burton looked from the open window of the train and across the sea to where Saint Michael's Mount towered above the surf lapping around its solid rock base. It was high water and the stone path which visitors used to walk to the island was completely hidden beneath the tumbling waves.

The train creaked and groaned and its speed decreased as it neared the end of its journey. When it finally came to rest a short distance from the buffers in Penzance Station, Zac, with luggage in tow, stepped onto the station platform and waved to Lottie Burton, his grandmother, as she walked quickly towards him, her face set in a broad grin. When the two met they hugged each other in an affectionate embrace.

"It's great to be back, Gran and I'm really, really excited about seeing your house and of course the friends I made here last summer," He smiled, "I think they're even looking forward to seeing me."

"And we're really excited about having you to stay with us, Zac. We've not had any guests since we moved to Cornwall. Although I suppose it was only seven months ago."

"It seems longer than that since we waved you off. Don't tell him I said so but Dad misses you. Well, he misses your cherry cakes."

Lottie laughed. "I'm not sure whether that's a compliment or not."

"It's a compliment," said Zac, emphatically.

"In that case I'll make him one for you to take home with you but that's not for a while yet so you'll have to remind me nearer the time."

"No problem, I'll do that."

"So did you have a good journey?" They reached the end of the platform and walked towards the exit.

"Yeah, it was brill especially running alongside the sea in Devon and this last bit's pretty cool too. I managed the Underground alright as well. Not bad for a country boy, eh?"

"No not bad at all but then you're young and youngsters today have a lot more confidence than we did in my day. Well, more confidence than me anyway although to be fair travelling alone wouldn't have bothered Hetty at any stage in her life."

"How is Auntie Hetty?" Zac asked, as they stepped out into the sunshine.

"Oh, she's fine and really happy at the moment because the workmen started on the loft conversion yesterday. Well, actually it was started last week when the joinery firm put in the specially made staircase. It's all very exciting and we're both longing to see it done. It'll make such a difference to us and then you'll all be able to come and stay at once. You, your mum and dad and your sisters."

Zac sniggered as they walked across the car park. "I actually think Vicky and Kate are quite envious that I get to stay here first but of course they wouldn't admit it."

As they reached a small yellow car, Lottie unlocked its doors. Zac put his luggage into the boot and then climbed into the passenger seat beside his grandmother. "And you're driving now," he said, "Well done you."

"Thank you, I must admit I really enjoy driving and I'm ever so glad your Auntie Hetty made me learn. She made me get a mobile phone too and learn to use her laptop." She chuckled, "I'm very proud of my driving though because I passed first time whereas poor Het took three attempts but I don't dwell on that fact because she's a very good driver and I think it'll take me a few years to have her confidence." She started the engine, reversed and then drove towards the car park exit. "You're seventeen now aren't you, Zac? Have you started driving lessons yet?"

"No, because still being at school means I don't have any income. Mum and Dad offered to pay for lessons but I don't want to take their hard earned cash. Things will be different in September though because Dad's got me a Saturday job at the supermarket where he works and I'll be able to do extra hours at half term and during the school holidays."

"So will you start learning in September then?"

"That's the plan. For now I just want to pass my test and get that over and done with, then when I'm older and working full time I'll get a car. The insurance is so expensive for us young chaps and often costs more than the first car."

Lottie paused briefly to concentrate on the busy roundabout.

"Yes, you must learn, Zac, it'll open up a whole new world for you. The chap next door to us is a driving instructor and he's very good. It's a pity he's not a bit nearer you."

Hetty was in the front garden sweeping the tarmac when Lottie arrived with Zac. Albert was with her chasing dandelion seed heads blowing in from the grass verge on the opposite side of the road.

"Welcome to Primrose Cottage." Hetty leaned the broom against the garage wall and hugged her great-nephew as he stepped from the car. Albert seeing a new face stopped chasing the seed heads and sniffed Zac's legs instead.

"Blimey, Auntie Het, you're really skinny now." Zac was clearly impressed.

"That's sweet of you to say so. I must admit I feel much better for it and can tackle aerobics pretty well as much as the youngsters." She cast a loving look at Albert. "I have a lot more energy too which is just as well as this young rascal does like his walks."

"You actually look like twins now you're the same size and Grandma has the same colour hair." Zac stooped down to pet Albert who seemed desperate to make his acquaintance.

Lottie touched her brown locks. "You noticed."

"Of course, but I didn't know whether or not I ought to mention it."

"I got your grandmother to dye her hair last New Year's Eve for the fancy dress and she liked it so much that she's been dyeing it ever since. I'm really proud of her."

Lottie took Zac's case from the boot. "I'm proud of you too, and Sid. Do you know, Zac, they lost a total of four and a half stone between them and raised five hundred and sixteen pounds for charity."

"Wow! Well done, but who's Sid?"

Lottie closed the boot. "He's a plumber and he's currently working in our new shower room. He's a smashing bloke, you'll like him and Basil and Mark too. They're doing the building type work. You know, putting up stud walls and so forth. They finished the windows today so it's already taking shape."

After being shown his room, Zac explored the house and then went out into the garden where his grandmother was unpegging washing from the line.

"He's arrived safe and sound then," called a deep, male voice.

Lottie looked towards the wall where a man's head and shoulders were visible over the top. "You've grown," she laughed.

"Sorry, I'm being nosy. We're out here having a barbecue, you see, and I heard young Zac's voice so jumped up onto the bench to take a peep."

Lottie dropped the last item of washing into the laundry basket. "Zac, this is our next door neighbour, Alex, and Alex as you've already realised, this is my grandson, Zac."

Zac reached up and shook Alex's hand. "Are you the neighbour who is a driving instructor?"

"Yes, but only part time. The wife and I run the antique shop in the village as well."

"The wife also has a name and it's Ginny," rebuked a female voice as a face appeared alongside Alex. "Please forgive my husband, Lottie, for his appalling bad manners." She tutted, "Spying on one's neighbours is sneaky, Alex."

"But forgivable," insisted Lottie, "and if the truth be known, I think it's something most people will be guilty of at least once in a lifetime."

Zac was allocated the smallest of the three bedrooms on the north side of the house overlooking the back garden and the countryside beyond. Knowing his great aunt and grandmother liked everything to be neat and tidy, he put his clothes and belongings away in the chest of drawers once he'd unpacked and tucked his case beneath the single bed. He then sat down and sent messages on his phone to Emma and Kyle, his friends in Cornwall, and then to his parents to let them know he'd arrived safe and sound.

In the evening Hetty, Lottie and Zac walked down to the Crown and Anchor for a meal and so that Zac could meet up with Kyle for a game or two of pool. The pub was busy with holidaymakers, many with children also dining and a few locals, mostly men, who sat on high stools alongside the bar.

After their meal, when Zac went off to play pool, Hetty and Lottie took their drinks out onto the terrace which overlooked the beach. The sea was flat-calm: there was not a breath of wind and the evening felt a little chilly for the sun had moved round to the side of the building leaving the terrace in part shade.

By ten o'clock, Zac was feeling tired; his eyes felt heavy and he could not stop yawning so they left the pub and crossed the road into Long Lane. Zac was still yawning when Lottie unlocked the door of Primrose Cottage. "It's the sea air to blame," she said, "For some reason it's tiring but you'll soon get used to it."

"Yeah, I remember that when we were here last summer and I suppose you can't get much further from the sea than Northamptonshire. Not in this country anyway."

Lottie nodded. "No, I suppose not."

"So have you made any plans for tomorrow?" Hetty asked, as they went inside the house.

Zac shook his head. "No, I'm here for six weeks so there's plenty of time to plan things once I'm settled in. Right now I just want to sleep so I don't think you'll see me very early tomorrow."

Zac yawned repeatedly as he closed the door of his room, undressed and climbed into bed. It had after all been a very long day, but enjoyable and the first he hoped of many. Before he turned off the bedside lamp, he checked his phone to see if there were any messages from home; he then laid his head on the pillow. On the ceiling, several cracks ran through the plaster and to amuse himself he looked to see if he could make out images in the faint lines. He laughed when he decided that the biggest cluster of cracks resembled Dodge, his best mate at school. With a smile on his face, he turned off the light and promptly fell asleep.

Chapter Two

Zac was woken the following morning by noises in the attic; feet shuffling across the bare floorboards, muffled voices and music which he assumed came from a radio. Keen to see what was being done he forgot about having a lie-in and instead grabbed his clothes, took a quick shower and went downstairs.

"It sounds like your blokes are here and working already," said Zac, looking at the clock which said half past eight.

Hetty glanced over her shoulder and smiled as she took milk from the fridge. "Yes, they're very reliable and always here at eight o'clock sharp."

"Basil and Mark, that is," Lottie added, "Sid comes separately and so his times vary. In fact he won't be here 'til later today because he's gone to sort out a leaking pipe for someone in the village."

"So what happened to your lie-in?" Hetty asked as she stirred milk into two mugs of strong tea.

"Inquisitiveness," replied Zac, "and the fact that once I'm awake I find it difficult to get back to sleep especially when it's light."

"I thought as much. Come on," commanded Hetty, as she lifted up the mugs, "and I'll introduce you to Basil and Mark before you have your breakfast."

The new stairs which led up to the loft from the landing were narrower than the main staircase and uncarpeted hence the sound of their feet on the treads told Basil and Mark of their imminent arrival.

"Sounds like tea's coming," they heard a voice call from above, "best move that bag, lad. We don't want the ladies falling over it and spilling our brew."

When they reached the top Zac saw a young lad not much older than himself dragging a large bag of tools into a corner. He nodded to the lad, stepped from the staircase and looked around the open space. "It's much bigger than I thought it would be and I see you've got the floor down already," Zac tapped the wooden boards with his foot.

"Zac, this is Basil," explained Hetty as she placed the two mugs on top of a box.

Basil shook Zac's hand.

"And this young urchin is Mark," teased Basil. He nodded towards the lad who stood with his hands in his pockets.

"I think you two woke Zac up this morning," tutted Hetty, "He was going to have a lie-in."

"Whoops, sorry about that," laughed Basil, "but not easy keeping quiet on bare boards. They were already down by the way which saved quite a bit of work although Sid'll have to take them up in that corner to do the plumbing." He pointed to the side of the loft which was above the bathroom.

"Sid being the plumber," Hetty reminded him.

"And you'll like him," chuckled Lottie, having come up to join them, "he's quite a character and extremely good at his job."

"So there's going to be a shower room up here as well as two bedrooms. I can't wait to see it done."

"Yes, and look at these views, Zac, aren't they wonderful?" Lottie pointed to the two new dormer windows which looked out towards the coast.

"Fantastic," he agreed, "I can see why you chose to live here."

Sid arrived just after lunch having repaired the leaking pipe. He was a man of medium height, in his forties and a bachelor who had never been enticed into marriage; he was also relatively new to the village having only arrived in late November the previous year. He lived in a modest two bedroomed semi-detached bungalow in Honeysuckle Close near to his friend, Bernie the Boatman.

Shortly after Sid's arrival, Emma one of the girls with whom Zac had made friends last summer called round to see him. She gave him a hug.

"It's brilliant to have you back, Zac. I saw Kyle on my way up here and he said you were in the pub last night and so had a few games of pool. I was baby-sitting so didn't get out but we can meet up again tonight, if you like."

"Great, I shall look forward to it."

"Would you like a cup of tea, Emma?" Hetty called from the kitchen. "I'm just about to make one for the chaps upstairs now Sid's here."

Emma peeped round the kitchen door. "No thank you, I've just had a cup with Chloe. I called in there before I came here because she wanted me to see the last bedroom that's been decorated before it's occupied tomorrow."

"Is that the same Chloe that used to own the café you worked in during the holidays?" Zac asked.

"That's right and she's now next door in Tuzzy-Muzzy. She sold the café back in March because she fancied a change."

"And how is she liking running a guest house?" Lottie asked. "I've not seen her since the busy part of the holiday season got underway but know she seemed happy enough a while back and she had a busy half term week in May."

"She's loving it because she said once breakfast is over and the rooms are all done she pretty well has the rest of the day to herself. In fact she thinks she might need to find a hobby but that would be more for the winter because she has the garden to keep tidy at present although Alfie pops over and helps if there's any heavy work to do and of course Colin does his fair share."

"Who are Alfie and Colin?" Zac asked, keen to know who everyone was.

"Alfie is Chloe's brother, he's a gardener and he lives in Penzance. Colin is Chloe's husband, he's a train driver and so works irregular hours."

Zac chuckled. "A train driver. Wow! Every boy's dream."

In the evening, Zac left his aunt and grandmother watching television and walked down to the Crown and Anchor where he met Kyle and Emma in the games area.

"Who's that bloke over there?" Zac nodded towards a young man standing at the bar chatting to someone he knew to be Bernie the Boatman, a man in his fifties who took out sea anglers in his boat. "I only ask because he was walking just ahead of me down Long Lane so I thought he might live in Blackberry Way somewhere near Gran and Auntie Het."

Kyle turned to see to whom Zac was referring. "Oh him, yes, he does. He and his wife are renting Fuchsia Cottage from old Tommy Thomas. He's called Luke, but I don't know any more about him than that because he's not been in the village long."

Emma sat down on a stool and took a sip of lager. "He's Luke Burleigh. I don't think I've ever spoken to him but his wife's called Natalie and I only know that because Mum mentioned her. Apparently she's keen to join the aerobics classes that Mum and a friend of hers run."

"Aerobics. Auntie Het mentioned that had helped her lose weight," said Zac.

"Yes, and your aunt still goes and so does your grandma. The classes have stopped now though until September because several people will be away over the next few weeks."

Zac glanced into the main bar. "I think by the time I've got to recognise everyone it'll be time to go home. There are loads of unfamiliar faces in here tonight."

"Don't worry. Lots of them are holidaymakers and they'll change several times over while you're here." Kyle picked up his pool cue. "Ready for a game?"

"Yes. I'll pay and you set the balls up." Zac took some change from the pocket of his jeans and placed it on the side of the pool table. "So who runs the café now that Chloe's moved to the guest house?" He asked Emma as Kyle collected the yellow and red balls.

"Taffeta and it's now called Taffeta's Tea Shoppe."

"Taffeta," repeated Zac, "Strange name. I take it you're not working there this summer."

Emma shook her head. "No, this will be my last long summer holiday as next June I'll have finished my college course and so will have started work. For that reason I decided to make the most of this summer and be foot loose and fancy free."

"So do you have a job lined up then?"

"Yes, but there's a bit of nepotism involved and so for now I'll say no more."

"She won't even tell me," teased Kyle, as he chalked the tip of his cue, "and we've known each other for ever."

"Point taken," said Zac, "So how about you then, Kyle. When do you finish uni?"

"Next year, same as Emma and before you ask, no, I don't know what I'm going to do then."

"Yeah, same as me then. I'm currently doing my A-Levels but I've no idea what my next move will be, but I've got a year to think about it anyway." He picked up his cue. "Are you still doing the bread round in the holidays? I meant to ask you last night but forgot."

Kyle shook his head. "No, I gave that up at the end of last summer. I work here now on the bar and I must admit I rather enjoy it."

"Oh, wow, that must be fun. So how many days do you work?"

"I have flexible hours but it's usually three lunchtimes during the week and then a couple of evenings. I don't have set days because things change from week to week and so the rota depends a lot on who is available to work."

Chapter Three

When Zac sat up in bed the following morning, he saw there were specks of white powder on the duvet cover at the bottom of his bed. He looked up to the ceiling. The cracks he had looked at on his first night in Cornwall no longer bore any resemblance to his friend Dodge and part of the plaster was hanging loose. Zac sprang from his bed suddenly afraid that the whole ceiling might fall down. He quickly dressed and dashed downstairs to report the situation to his grandmother and aunt. He found them in the kitchen, Lottie making a cake and Hetty loading up the washing machine.

After viewing the ceiling, Hetty called up the new staircase to the loft and asked Basil for his advice. He came down and so did Sid the plumber.

"Oh dear," tutted Basil, removing his shoes and standing on Zac's bed. He touched the loose piece of plaster and it came away in his hand causing everyone to step out onto the landing in case anymore of the ceiling fell.

"Looks like we might have to take the whole ceiling down," said Basil, shutting the door to contain the dust. "It's no good trying to repair it as there are too many cracks and you'd be better with a plasterboard one anyway." He glanced towards the doors on the opposite side of the landing. "Have you checked the other rooms to see if they're okay?"

"No, we didn't think of that," confessed Hetty, "I'll go and have a look."

Lottie went with her and they were happy to report that their own bedrooms and the bathroom were fine.

Basil looked relieved. "Good, we've obviously dislodged it banging around. These old lathe and plaster ceilings are no doubt the originals. I'm amazed they stay up as long as they do in these old places."

Lottie bit her bottom lip. "Oh dear, it looks like you're going to have to move out then, Zac. You can't stay in there with the ceiling unsafe."

"That's okay and I don't mind sleeping on the settee."

Hetty stroked his cheek fondly. "Ow, bless you and you've only been here for a couple of days."

"I'll take the ceiling down as well if you like. It can be my contribution to my keep while I'm here. I know what to do because I helped Dad replace the ceiling in our hallway back home."

"That'd be a great help if you did," said Basil as he opened the door to see if the dust had settled, "and I'll order some extra sheets of plasterboard when I'm next at the builder's merchants."

The dust had settled and as they all went into the room to survey the damage, Lottie pointed to the hole left by the fallen plaster. "What's that I can see? It looks like a box or something."

Hetty squinted. "You're right, it does. I wonder what it can be."

Basil jumped up on the bed again, reached up and touched the corner of something dark brown in colour. "Hmm, I don't know what it is." He gave it a little push and more plaster fell. "Whoops, better not try to get it from here until you've cleared the room out or the whole ceiling might come down." He climbed off the bed.

Hetty sighed, clearly disappointed. "Oh well, I don't suppose it'll hurt us having to wait until the ceiling's gone although I must admit I'd like to know what the box thing is now."

Lottie nodded. "And so would I."

"That's not a problem then," declared Sid, who was also intrigued, "We can lift the floorboards in the loft to find out what it is from up there."

Basil brushed dust from his sleeve. "Good idea, Sid. I must admit I'm rather curious too because the boards in the attic don't look as if they've been disturbed since they were put down and I reckon that was a fair while ago." He moved towards the new staircase, "Come on then, let's go up and a take a look."

With the aid of a crow bar, Basil lifted a board in the area over the spare bedroom. There was nothing to see. As he lifted another, part of the brown item they had spotted in Zac's room was just visible wedged between the beams. Basil lifted more boards.

"A pair of bloke's shoes," said Mark, looking over Basil's shoulder, "and they're dead old fashioned."

Sid reached down and lifted the shoes up. "Well I never. Leather soles. They're pretty old as well."

"There's a coat too and it looks like that would have belonged to a man as well." Basil unfolded the tweed bundle, passed it to Lottie and then lifted another board.

"It's a suitcase," exclaimed Hetty, "and an old suitcase at that. I remember Dad had a similar one."

"But Dad's was much bigger," said Lottie, as she laid the coat down on the Workmate.

Basil leaned forwards and carefully, so as not to knock away more of the ceiling, slid the suitcase out from where it was squeezed between the beams and lifted it onto the floorboards. He tried to open it but both catches had seized up. Sid came to the rescue with a can of WD 40. After a few minutes the catches began to move and Basil opened up the lid.

The suitcase was full to the brim and on top were a few items of clothing, neatly folded. Beneath them was a model of a boat carved in wood and painted blue. Next to it was a cine camera and two reels of film. A small bag of men's toiletries was tucked in a corner and a wallet containing two one pound notes, a ten shilling note, pre-decimal coins and an identity card lay beneath it along with a pocket watch. In an envelope was a black and white photograph of two young men standing on a beach beside a boat. One of the men was in Army uniform, the other wore a dark jumper and a flat cap and from his mouth dangled a cigarette. Basil turned the picture over but there was no name or date on the back.

"Bernie would be the person to ask about that boat," said Sid, looking at the picture over Basil's shoulder, "that's assuming the photo was taken here in Pentrillick."

"You're right, he would," Hetty agreed. She knelt down beside Basil. "What's the name on the identity card? I can't read it without my glasses."

"David Tregear, born 1912 and unmarried. It says his occupation was Train Driver so he might be the chap smoking the fag. His address is the Pentrillick Hotel." Basil handed the card to Hetty, "I suppose it was one issued during the Second World War. What do you think?"

"Definitely because they were still issued once the war was over and I still have mine."

"There's something in here," said Zac, who was looking at the old overcoat and had put his hand inside one of its pockets. "Well, I never it's a postcard."

Sid glanced at the card. "And it looks to me like a wartime issue because there's no stamp in the corner."

"Probably from the chap in the old photo wearing uniform then," suggested Basil.

Hetty's fingers twitched. "How exciting. What does it say? Who is it from? Please read it, Zac."

"It's dated January 2nd 1942 and is addressed to Mr David Tregear at the Pentrillick Hotel. It says: *Dear Dave, I'm missing you mate and wish I could be home with you and the rest of the family. Dream of Cornwall often and long to swim in the sea again and watch the sun setting over Mounts Bay. Hope Old Jimmy's behaving. Hope you're all well and I hope to see you all again soon. Meanwhile, pray for me, Dave. Pray for us all. Love to Mum, Peter. x"*

For thirty seconds no-one spoke as the words sank in.

It was Lottie who broke the silence. "I do hope he survived and came home and swam in the sea again."

"And watched the sun setting over Mounts Bay," whispered Hetty.

Sid scratched his head. "Yeah, same here but what I want to know is why all this stuff's up here and hidden as well?"

"And I wonder who old Jimmy is," reflected Zac.

Lottie brushed a tear from her cheek. "Two good questions, but at least we know that the Dave who received the postcard is definitely David Tregear and he was a train driver."

Mark looked serious. "Probably a dog. My next door neighbours have a dog called Jimmy. He's a Collie."

"You chump," laughed Basil, "Trust you to bring us back to earth."

"Perhaps David Tregear whoever he might be was killed during the war and someone put his personal things up here because it was too painful to see them," suggested Hetty.

"Well he was still here in January 1942 when he got the postcard from Peter, whoever Peter might be," said Lottie, "so if he was killed, and I sincerely hope he wasn't, it must have been after that date."

Hetty picked up the identity card. "I'm just trying to think. According to this he was a train driver so I wonder if for that reason he might have been exempt from conscription. I know people in several occupations were."

"Yes, most likely," declared Sid, "My uncle was a train driver and he never went to war although having said that I know some who worked on the railway did but they might not have been drivers."

Basil scratched his head. "Well, for the sake of argument let's assume David did go to war and was killed and his things were put up here because it was too painful to see them. I mean, I can understand someone wanting to do that. But what I can't understand is why it was necessary to hide everything beneath the floorboards when it'd all be out of sight just by being in the attic. If you see what I mean."

"We shall have to investigate," Hetty spoke with a look of determination on her face, "The trouble is though I've no idea where to start with so little to go on."

Lottie laughed. "We could do with Psychic Sid's help here."

"Oh yes," Mark agreed, "My Mum had her fortune told by him at the Christmas Wonderland. He told her she would get some money she wasn't expecting and so she bought a Lottery ticket and won twenty five pounds."

Hetty smiled. "Hmm, a good prediction but not exactly a life-changing amount."

"Well, Mum was dead chuffed and said he was amazing." Mark frowned, "I wonder what happened to him but then I suppose he went off up-country with the rest of the fair people."

"Or perhaps he became a plumber," teased Hetty, nodding in Sid's direction.

"No way," chortled Basil as he cottoned on, "You're not a psychic, are you, Sid?"

"Well," Sid hesitated, "yes and no. That is I was for a while but then went back to my original trade which is plumbing."

"So were you any good? Or should I say, are you any good?"

Sid shook his head. "No I was rubbish."

Mark looked confused. "But if you're Psychic Sid you must be good because Mum said so and she knows all about that stuff because when she was a kid her next door neighbour used to read the tealeaves."

"So what else did Psychic Sid say to your mum?" Basil asked.

"I can't remember but I'll ask her when I go home."

"Well if Psychic Sid can't help us," chuckled Hetty, "we'll need to think of a more down to earth way of finding out more about David Tregear."

"Why don't you go and have a look round the churchyard," suggested Zac. "I mean, if the bloke is dead, which I expect he would be by now anyway, then he'd be buried there somewhere so we might be able to learn something about him."

"Now that is a good idea," said Lottie, "Well done, Zac, and at least we'd know if he died during the war."

"Although if David died overseas then he may well be buried there," sighed Basil, "lots of our young men never got back to be buried at home. I always find that rather sad."

"And for many in the Navy their grave is the ocean bed," tutted Sid.

"It's still worth us looking in the churchyard," insisted Lottie, "because even if David isn't there, there may well be other Tregears."

"Well, there's only one way to find out," reasoned Hetty, scrambling to her feet, "Let's go right now. Will you come as well, Zac? The more pairs of eyes, the better and yours are a lot more efficient than mine and your grandma's."

"Yes, I'd love to, but I'd like some breakfast first because I'm starving."

Hetty and Lottie walked down to the churchyard with Zac who had Albert on his lead, for the little dog had taken to the sisters' young visitor and followed him around the house whenever he could.

"I suppose the best thing to do is look for graves from the nineteen forties and then search that area," suggested Lottie, glancing over the rows and rows of headstones, "it's no good looking before then because we know he was still alive when war broke out because he had an identity card."

"And he was still alive in 1942 when he got the postcard," Zac added.

"Of course," tutted Lottie, "silly me."

"Well, all I hope is that David Tregear had a headstone," muttered Hetty, "because not everyone does."

"Shall we split up?" Zac asked, "Then whoever finds the right area can call the others over."

"Good idea," Hetty pointed to three trees, "I'll go and make a start over there."

It was Lottie who found graves from the right era. She beckoned Zac and Hetty to join her.

"Thankfully most are quite legible," she announced, "so hopefully we'll find what we're looking for without too much effort."

Half an hour later, Hetty came across a grave of interest. "Come and look at this," she cried, "It's not for David Tregear but for someone called Peter so they might be related." She lowered her voice, "Oh dear, he's probably the Peter who sent the postcard."

"Oh, please no," cried Lottie, "not Peter who longed to swim in the sea again and see the sunset."

Zac read the inscription on the large white ornate headstone: "*In Loving Memory of Peter Tregear, age 30, beloved son of Florence and Frank Tregear. Died February 7th 1942 from injuries inflicted while fighting for King and Country. RIP.*"

Hetty sighed. "Poor soul."

Lottie couldn't speak.

"I'm just trying to remember the information in the identity card we found," said Hetty, trying to be practical, " Would I be right in thinking that David Tregear was born in 1912?"

"Yes, he was," Lottie sobbed, "because I remember it was the same year that our dad was born."

"In which case, Peter Tregear buried here and David Tregear whose belongings we've found in the attic were born in the same year."

"Oh yes, you're right, Het. I wonder if they were cousins." Lottie dried her eyes.

"They could have been brothers," suggested Zac.

"No, not if they were born in the same year," chuckled Hetty.

Zac tutted loudly. "They could have been twins."

Lottie laughed. "Oh yes, good point, Zac. Your aunt and I of all people should have thought of that."

Hetty looked sheepish but was glad to see that her sister had cheered up. "Come on, let's see if we can find David."

"I've found another Tregear," called Zac, instantly as he took two steps along the path between the rows of graves, "this one is for Frank Tregear so he must be the Frank mentioned on Peter's headstone."

"And so he is Peter's father," said Lottie as she read the inscription. "And he died in 1915, so that would have been during the First World War." She looked at the graves on either side of Frank. "No sign of Florence though which seems odd because husbands and wives are usually buried together."

"Yes, but I daresay she lived for a good many more years after she lost Frank," reasoned Hetty. "I mean, the poor bloke was only twenty nine when he died so Florence was probably even younger and may even have re-married."

Lottie tutted. "What a terrible thing war is."

"Do you have any paper and a pen on you, Lottie?" Hetty asked, "Because I think we need to write these names and dates down as they might well be part of the puzzle and there's no way my poor old brain will be able to remember them."

"I definitely have a pen but not sure about paper." Lottie looked through the contents of her handbag and found an old shopping receipt. "This is the best I can do." She handed pen and paper to Hetty.

"Why don't we look on the war memorial," suggested Zac, as Hetty wrote down names and dates, "Because even if David did die overseas his name will be on that."

"War memorial," Hetty looked confused, "Is there one in Pentrillick?"

Zac chuckled. "Yes, it's over there." He pointed to the tall granite edifice standing by the churchyard's front boundary wall and cordoned off with a chain draped between wooden posts.

"Well I never," laughed Hetty, "how many times have I walked past that and not seen it?"

"Lots," smiled Lottie, "but don't worry because I'd not noticed it either. That is to say I've seen it but hadn't realised what it was."

Standing in front of the memorial they read through the names of those killed in action during both world wars and later conflicts but there was only one Tregear and that was Peter.

"No mention of Peter's father Frank even though he died in 1915," said Hetty, "so perhaps he didn't go to war then after all. I wonder why not."

"Probably because he wasn't a well man or he was a conscientious objector," reasoned Lottie, "Or maybe he was a doctor or a farmer. People with several occupations were exempt. But whatever the reason the poor man died young if he was only twenty nine,"

"Yes, of course and it doesn't matter anyway because he died long before 1942 and so will not help our investigations."

"And," reasoned Lottie, "it looks as though David didn't go to war either."

"Or if he did he survived the horrors and came home," whispered Hetty.

Zac frowned. "But whether or not he went to war doesn't really matter because the real mystery is, why was his suitcase hidden away in your attic?"

Hetty tucked the piece of paper in her pocket on which names and dates were written. "And that, Zac, is exactly what we intend to find out."

Chapter Four

Upstairs in his bedroom, Zac was taking down the old ceiling; the furniture from the room had already been removed and was carefully stacked in the dining room which was seldom used.

Meanwhile, in the sitting room, newlyweds and pensioners, Tommy and Kitty Thomas, friends of the sisters who lived at the far end of Blackberry Way in a cottage called Meadowsweet, were looking through the treasures from the attic.

"The name on this identity card is David Tregear," said Hetty, "Does that name mean anything to you, Kitty?"

Kitty took the card from Hetty and opened it up. "David Tregear," she shook her head, "I don't recall ever hearing mention of that name or the name Tregear for that matter. And his address is the Pentrillick Hotel. That seems odd."

"Precisely. Why would a train driver be living in a hotel?"

"Perhaps he lived there when the card was issued and then moved here," suggested Tommy, "Must be something like that otherwise why would his belongings be in your attic."

Kitty shook her head. "Good point, Tom, but I don't recall any Tregears ever living along here, but then I wasn't born 'til after the war so they might have gone before my time."

"There's a postcard here too from someone called Peter," Lottie took the card from the suitcase and handed it to Kitty, "And we have every reason to believe that he's the chap in the photograph wearing the uniform and that he died in 1942. We know this because we found his grave in the churchyard."

"We're also pretty certain that Peter and David were brothers," Hetty added, "I just wish there was a way of finding out for sure."

"I think you ought to have a word with Alex next door," proposed Tommy, admiring the carved boat, "He's not local to this village but he's keen on history and so he might know how to get some answers to your questions."

"That's an excellent idea," Hetty agreed, "I'll look out for him when he and Ginny get back from their antique shop which is usually just before six."

Zac came down from his bedroom. "Ceiling's gone," he announced, stepping into the sitting room and leaving behind a trail of white footprints, "Have you got any old bags or boxes because I need something to put the old plaster and lathes in."

Lottie gasped in horror. Zac's hair was white as were his forehead and eyebrows which had escaped protection from the scarf he'd worn across his mouth and nose. "Oh, Zac, you do look comical," she giggled.

Hetty took a picture on her phone and then showed it to him.

Zac laughed. "Send it to Dad so he can see that I'm making myself useful."

"Good idea, and then you can ring him later and tell him what we found in the attic."

"Ah yes, that reminds me, I found something else." Zac dashed from the room and ran up the stairs two at a time. When he returned he held in his hand an old discoloured pillowslip. "I think you might like what's in here." He handed the pillowslip to Lottie who was nearest the door. "It must have been tucked between the beams like the shoes and coat because it fell down when I pulled away part of the ceiling."

Lottie cautiously peeped inside the pillowslip; in the bottom sat an old teddy bear. She pulled him out. "Poor old thing. He must have been up there with the suitcase all this time." She passed the bear to her sister who had moved closer to see the latest find.

Hetty sat him on the palm of her hand and straightened his ears. "Well whoever owned him must have loved him dearly because his fur is very worn in places."

"I suppose he must have belonged to David," Lottie half-smiled, "Oh, little bear, if only you could talk."

By evening the lathes had been burned at the end of the garden and the old plaster lay in a heap while they decided how to dispose of it. The room had been cleaned and vacuumed and was ready for the plasterboard to be put in place. The carpet which the sisters had planned to replace anyway, was neatly folded in the garage.

"Are you going out tonight?" Lottie asked Zac, as they sat in the sitting room around a small dining table eating their dinner.

"No, there's a darts match on in the pub so we won't be able to use the pool table."

"In that case if you want you can join us for a game or two of Scrabble. Sid's coming round later as he does every Thursday and it'd be nice if there were four of us."

"Yeah, sounds good. I sometimes play Scrabble with Mum and Dad and often beat them, especially Dad who Mum tells off because he makes words up."

Lottie tutted. "Oh dear, I remember your dad cheating at Ludo when he and your Auntie Barbara were youngsters. He'd move along extra places when she wasn't looking. Mind you if she caught him all hell broke loose."

Hetty chuckled. "Hope you don't take after him then, Zac?"

"No, I'm not a cheat in any way. Mum always says cheats never prosper and I think there's a lot to be said for that. Although to be fair to Dad he's really honest at everything else and would never do anyone down."

"Anyway," said Hetty, who was sitting by the table close to the window, "it'll be more fun if there are four of us playing but I must warn you, Zac, that Sid is very good." From the corner of her eye she saw movement outside which caused her to scowl. Walking along the road whistling with both hands tucked in the pockets of his jeans was the tenant of Fuchsia Cottage.

"Humph, there goes surly Burleigh again and no doubt off to the pub. I'd like to know what he's up to. I've seen him quite a lot in the daytime recently, so why isn't he at work?"

"Perhaps he has some time off," suggested Lottie, "not everyone goes away for a holiday and he's probably just enjoying being in Cornwall."

Zac looked at his aunt. "Why don't you like him?"

"Because he's a misery," Hetty retorted.

"He didn't sound like a misery," reasoned Zac, impishly, "People who whistle are usually quite happy and I saw him laughing in the pub the other night."

Lottie chuckled. "He has a point, Het, and to be fair we've only witnessed him being grumpy once."

"So what did he do?" Zac persisted.

"Albert was in the garden minding his own business when Burleigh walked by. Being a good dog Albert barked and Burleigh said in a very aggressive tone, Shut up mutt."

Zac decided it was best not to comment for he knew better than to disagree with his elders especially when said elders were relations and female to boot.

"So what time will Sid be here?" he asked, knowing he was on safer ground.

"About half seven," said Lottie. "She looked at the clock, "And I see it's nearly that now so we'd better get the table cleared and get the board out."

Sid arrived promptly at half past seven with his usual four cans of lager. As he took a seat at the table Hetty went to the kitchen and came back with a bottle of wine and some glasses.

"Would you like a glass of wine, Zac?" Hetty asked.

He shook his head. "No thanks I'm not very keen on it."

"You're welcome to one of my cans," said Sid, "I never drink all four because I like to keep my wits about me."

"In that case, yes please," Zac replied.

While drinks were being poured, Lottie showed Sid the teddy bear.

"Well, I never," he chuckled, "You're a bit of a tatty head, aren't you, mate?"

Lottie tutted. "Don't be beastly, Sid. Poor little bear."

"I think anyone would be a bit tatty if they'd been lying under floorboards in an attic for the past seventy five years," joked Zac.

Sid took the bear from Lottie and straightened his thin red tie. "So, have you given him a name?"

Lottie and Hetty both shook their heads.

"Perhaps he's old Jimmy," suggested Zac.

"Hmm, might well be," agreed Hetty, "but I think he looks more like a Fred."

Lottie laughed. "Well, if we're making wild guesses I'll go for Pilchard as they were quite prolific back when this little chap would have been new."

Sid shook his head. "No, I reckon you're all wrong and my money goes on Saffron Bun."

"Another good name," laughed Lottie, "but as we all have different ideas I think for now we'll just have to refer to him as the bear." She then placed him on the window sill so that he could watch the game of Scrabble.

When they were all seated at the table and the board was in place they each took it in turns to take seven tiles from a bag.

Lottie, whose turn it was to go first grumbled: "Mine are rubbish as usual." To the amusement of the others she put down THE.

Zac looked smug. "I can do much better because I have a six letter word but will have to use Grandma's E to achieve it." He laid down CLOSET.

Sid chuckled and rubbed his hands gleefully. "I can beat you, Zac because I'm going to use all my tiles and make an eight letter word." Using the L at the beginning in CLOSET he made the word SKELETON.

Hetty scowled. "Humph, very good, Sid but I don't think I've ever had such horrible letters." She laid down IN using the N in SKELETON.

Lottie laughed. "Looks like we ought to ditch the wine, Het, and drink lager."

"Skeleton in the closet," read Zac, "Is there a message there?"

Lottie's face turned white. "I hope not but the weird thing is, I felt I wasn't in control when I put down THE, especially as I can see a much better word now."

"Same here," Hetty agreed, "What on earth made me put down IN when I could have had SKINT?"

Sid laughed. "Perhaps your David Tregear is trying to tell us something."

"That's what I'm thinking," scowled Hetty, and she poured herself a bumper glass of wine, "and I don't think I like it."

Chapter Five

After breakfast on Saturday morning, Hetty hooked Albert's lead onto his collar and took him out for a walk leaving Lottie to dust and vacuum the sitting room and hallway, a chore they took turns to do.

The morning was dry, bright and sunny with a light wind blowing from the south east, so when Hetty reached the bottom of Long Lane she took a different route and turned right past the Crown and Anchor. The road led out of the village away from the coast towards Vince's garage and the A394 but Hetty had no intention of going that far. Instead, after passing the primary school, she climbed over a stile and into a meadow where cows grazed on the lush green grass. Because of the cattle, she kept Albert on his lead and followed the well-worn path across the field towards the sea where a wooden fence ran along the boundary separating the field from the coastal path beyond. When Hetty reached the fence she stopped and climbed the wooden struts to the top. The view was breathtaking. To her left was Pentrillick beyond which lay the Lizard Peninsula in the distance and to her right, just visible, were Saint Michael's Mount and the contour of Tol-Pedn. In order to go back by a different route, she climbed over the fence, jumped down on the opposite side and lifted Albert through the struts to join her. They then followed the coastal path back towards Pentrillick, past a row of coastguard cottages and then down a track which led onto the beach.

When she arrived back in Blackberry Way, Hetty noticed a woman nicely dressed in beige cotton trousers and a lightweight jacket. She was leaning on the gate opposite Primrose Cottage and appeared to be looking out over the village, to the coastline and the distant horizon.

"Good morning," said Hetty, cheerfully, as the woman turned on hearing footsteps, "beautiful day, isn't it?"

"Yes, yes, it is and this view is quite breath-taking. I think I could stand here admiring it for hours."

Hetty smiled. "It is and that's part of the reason why we bought our house. For the view, I mean."

"You live up here then?"

Hetty nodded towards Primrose Cottage. "Yes, that's my home which I share with my twin sister."

"Lucky you. I wish I lived here but unfortunately I live in the town and so have no view at all although to be fair my house is comfortable and I do have a beautiful secluded garden."

"Are you on holiday then?"

The woman stepped away from the gate. "Yes and I only arrived yesterday afternoon. I'm staying next door to you in the guest house."

"Tuzzy-Muzzy," said Hetty, "so we're neighbours."

"For a while, yes."

Hetty glanced around to see if there was anyone else nearby. "Would it be rude to ask if you're here on your own?"

"Not at all and yes I am. I'm here for a whole month so that I can have a nice long rest. I nursed my elderly mother for a long six months, you see. Sadly she's no longer with us now but her passing meant there was a lot to sort out, you know, selling her house and so forth. It was all very stressful and my partner, bless him, said I must get away and have some time to myself."

"That's very sweet of him but will he be alright on his own?"

"Yes, he's a barrister and has a lot of very good friends to help him out. Besides, he's also an accomplished cook and has fended for himself a lot already this year especially when my mother's health began to deteriorate."

"That's nice to hear and you chose Cornwall for your rest. Very wise of you."

"Yes, I thought it would be the perfect place to find peace and quiet."

"Fancy a coffee? You can meet my sister then."

"Well, yes, that would be lovely. Thank you."

"My name's Hetty, by the way, Hetty Tonkins."

"Pleased to make your acquaintance, Hetty. I'm Grace, Grace Dunkerley." She glanced down at Albert. "And who is this little fellow?"

Hetty introduced Grace to Albert and then they crossed the road.

"Please excuse any strange noises," urged Hetty, as they approached the house and she opened the door. "We're having a loft conversion done and so at times it can be quite noisy."

"A loft conversion. How exciting. I love making alterations to my house and decorating too."

Inside Primrose Cottage, Emma and Zac were making coffee for Sid, Basil and Mark.

"Care to make a couple more for your poor old aunt and this lady, Grace, who's staying next door?" called Hetty to the kitchen as she hung up Albert's lead.

"No problem," said Emma, "would Lottie like one too?"

"Yes please," replied Lottie who was in the sitting room, knitting, where she cast a quizzical look at her sister and Grace as they entered the room.

"Lottie, this is Grace and she's staying next door at Tuzzy-Muzzy for a few weeks, and Grace, this is my twin sister, Lottie."

"Pleased to meet you," Lottie stood up and shook hands with the visitor.

"Likewise and what a lovely bright room," remarked Grace as she glanced around, "I do like wooden floors they seem so much cosier than concrete."

"I agree, all the downstairs rooms are wooden except the kitchen which is solid and tiled. Sit down, Grace, anywhere you like," said Hetty as Emma came in with a tea tray. Grace sat at the table near to the window where the sunlight caused jewellery she was wearing to sparkle.

"I like your brooch," said Emma, admiringly as she handed Grace a mug of coffee, "It's quite unusual and what a beautiful shade of blue."

Grace lovingly touched the large brooch pinned on the lapel of her jacket. "Thank you, dear, it's very special to me. It used to belong to my grandmother, you see, and was a present to her from my grandfather on their first wedding anniversary. Sadly I never knew her because she died many years before I was born."

"Is it a dragonfly?" Lottie asked, squinting to focus better from where she sat on the opposite side of the room.

Grace nodded. "Yes, it is and I like to think of it as a lucky charm because in China people associate dragonflies with prosperity, harmony and as, I say, good luck."

"Really, I didn't know that," conceded Lottie.

"Nor me," agreed Hetty, "which is interesting because we're thinking of making a pond in our back garden so that it'll draw some wildlife. I had a small pond in my garden up-country and on several occasions it attracted dragonflies. They really are very beautiful."

"That's a lovely idea," Grace acknowledged, "I find the pond next door quite fascinating and sat beside it for some time yesterday afternoon watching the wildlife. I didn't see any dragonflies though but must have another look when I've time to spare." She laughed. "What a silly thing to say, I keep forgetting that I'm on holiday and have all the time in the world."

"Well if you want someone to dig a hole for the pond, Auntie Hetty, I'd be more than willing to do it," said Zac, sitting on the floor dunking chocolate digestive biscuits in his coffee and then licking off the melted chocolate.

"And I'll help too," smiled Emma, sitting down beside him, "I like doing physical work as it helps keep my weight down."

"Excellent," chortled Hetty, "two volunteers. You can start as soon as we've decided where to have it."

Chapter Six

On Sunday morning, the sisters' next door neighbour, Alex from Hillside called round to see Hetty and Lottie to tell them what he had so far discovered.

"I started by looking for the births of David and Peter Tregear and as you suggested they are indeed twins and were born in 1912."

"Twins, how wonderful," exclaimed Lottie, "I feel quite attached to them now."

"I thought you might. Anyway, my next search was for Frank Tregear because we already knew through his tombstone that he died in 1915 and was born in 1886. I've now looked at the 1911 census and according to that he and his wife Florence ran the Pentrillick Hotel. There is of course no mention of the David or Peter on the census as we've already established that they weren't born until 1912."

"The Tregears ran the hotel," gasped Hetty, "how fascinating. So that's why it's down as David's address on his identity card."

"That's what I thought," agreed Alex. "You learn something new every day. I'd never heard of the Tregears until you found the suitcase."

"But him living at the hotel doesn't explain why David's things were in our loft," reasoned Lottie.

"No, no it doesn't," agreed Alex, "but there is more. You see in 1925 Florence who was David and Peter's mother and a widow, married again and her new husband was a chap called Harold Berryman, a widower who was also born in 1886. I've established through looking at birth records that he had two children of his own from his previous marriage: a son called George born in 1917 and a daughter called Polly who was born in 1919."

"Ah, so do you think it's possible that the Berrymans lived here in this house?" Lottie asked.

"Yes, I do," said Alex, "and if that's the case then it's likely that David's things were put into the loft after his death by either George or Polly. They would after all have been step-siblings and probably very close because the Berryman children would only have been twelve and nine years old respectively when their father remarried and David and Peter would have been thirteen years old."

"So what happened to David?" Lottie asked. "I mean, if his things were put in the loft because the memory was too painful or something like that then he must have died."

"That's what I'm assuming," said Alex, "although it might be a little too presumptuous of me."

"But why put them in our loft and not somewhere at the hotel where his mother lived?" Hetty added.

"Good points which sadly I'm not able to answer. I mean it's possible that if David had died young then his stepbrother or stepsister may have offered to look after his things because the sight of them was too much for his mother Florence to bear. Remember she had after all already lost one of her sons due to the war. The problem is I can find no record of David Tregear dying either here in Cornwall or anywhere else for that matter and I've tried every year between 1940 and the year 2000."

"So what happened to him?" Lottie frowned, trying to think.

Alex shook his head. "I don't know but I've just remembered something else. I found a local newspaper article on-line regarding the funeral of Peter Tregear who you'll no doubt remember died in 1942 and his brother David is not listed amongst the mourners."

"What! So where was he?" Lottie asked. "I mean, why on earth would he not attend his twin brother's funeral?"

"I've no idea."

"Are there not any records of people who worked on the railway?" Hetty asked.

"Yes there are and I did look but sadly I could only find records that went back to 1947 when the railways were nationalised."

"In which case," sighed Hetty, "it looks as though he must have volunteered to go to war and died while on active service."

Lottie shook her head. "No, no, he didn't, Het. Remember his name's not on the war memorial so there's no way he died in conflict because if he had he'd definitely be there."

"Very good point," Alex agreed.

"Yes, yes, you're right and I'm just grasping at straws."

"Yet there must be a way of finding out what happened to him," reasoned Lottie, "I just can't think of one."

Hetty agreed. "Yes, we need answers but who can we ask? We've not come across anyone who remembers the Tregears and as far as we know neither David nor Peter had children anyway."

"It's just a thought," said Alex, "but it might be worth looking at the Berrymans. I mean, it's possible George or Polly had children and so if you can find their descendants they'll no doubt be able to put more pieces in the puzzle."

"Good thinking, Alex. Well done." Hetty's smile stretched from ear to ear.

"My pleasure. Now if you'll excuse me I must be off to give one of my pupils a driving lesson." He rose to leave.

Hetty nodded. "Yes you must get going but before you go, out of curiosity, do you know what line of work the Berrymans were in?"

Alex smiled broadly. "Harold was a funeral director. At least that's what it said on the 1911 census. George and Polly of course weren't born then so whether or not they took on the business in later years I've no idea. Perhaps you'll be able to find out."

"We'll do our best," chuckled Hetty, gleefully rubbing her hands together. "Thank you so much, Alex for your help. We really appreciate it."

"It's been a pleasure. I'll leave this piece of paper with the details of my little discoveries with you and please let me know if you find anything else of interest."

Hetty took the sheet of paper from Alex as she and Lottie walked with him to the front door. "We will," said Lottie, "In fact we shall get to work straight away, won't we, Het?"

"Yes, I'm raring to go and I think the first person we must visit is Kitty since she's lived here in Pentrillick all her life."

"Good choice," agreed Alex, as he stepped from the doorway, "and good luck."

"Berrymans," muttered Kitty, as Hetty and Lottie sat down beside her on a bench in the front garden of Meadowsweet, "Yes, I do remember a family of that name but can't really tell you much about them except that they had a son called Simon and lived in your house. Simon was of a similar age to me and I used to call for him and we'd walk to school together." She smiled at the memory, "He was so sweet when he was little. I can see him now in his short trousers and his clumpy shoes. He was a couple of weeks younger than me and so I took it upon myself to look after him. Sadly we lost touch when we were older and went to secondary school because he was in a different class to me. We each had our own friends anyway and I suppose that's life. I've not thought of him for years but just hearing mention of his name has brought it all flooding back."

"So you've no idea then where he is now?" Hetty asked.

"No, I haven't but if you go and see Maisie or Daisy at the charity shop you can ask them if they know anything. I can't remember which but one of them had a brother who was friends with him at secondary school. Probably even best friends. He was a handsome looking lad in those days, Simon that is, not Maisie or Daisy's brother, although I'm sure he was nice looking too. But Simon had lovely thick wavy black hair although I daresay it's a lot thinner now and several shades lighter as well." Kitty laughed, "He used to call me Kitty Kat."

"Wonderful," said Hetty, writing down the name Simon Berryman, "We'll look into that."

"How about the rest of the family?" Lottie asked. "Do you remember his father? Was his name George? And did he have an aunt called Polly."

Kitty drummed her fingers on the arm of the bench. "I don't remember an Aunt Polly at all and I don't know if Simon's father was called George. He was a stranger to me really because I didn't see him very often. To me he was Mr Berryman. He was an undertaker and I thought that was a bit sinister."

"An undertaker!" shrieked Hetty, "sounds like we're on the right track then because according to the 1911 census Harold Berryman, the man who we know to be George and Polly's father was a funeral director."

"How about Simon's mother?" Lottie asked, "Do you remember her at all?"

"Oh dear, yes, yes, I'd forgotten all about his mother. She was lovely and I saw her often when I called for Simon." Kitty sighed. "Sadly the poor lady died when Simon and I were very young. It was terrible. I believe she fell down the stairs or something like that. I remember my parents going to the funeral and I remember sometimes that Simon would cry in class when people spoke of their mothers."

"Poor Simon," said Hetty.

Kitty suddenly raised her hands. "Yes, he was called George. Mr Berryman that is because I remember now hearing my parents say poor George. You saying poor Simon, Hetty, triggered a memory."

Lottie sighed. "We seem to be unearthing one tragedy after another. First we find Peter Tregear died during the war and now George's wife died young. I hope there are going to be a few happy stories in our findings."

Kitty smiled. "Oh, I'm sure there will be and most families have a tale or two of woe to tell."

"So our next stop must be the charity shop," declared Hetty, in a practical manner, "and then if we can find out where Simon is we can perhaps pay him a visit."

Kitty grinned. "And I wish you luck. It'll be nice to know what he's doing although whatever path he took in life I daresay he'll be retired now."

"Time will tell," said Hetty, "and we'll either ring you or come and see you the minute we know what's what."

Grace called round in the afternoon and so they showed her the suitcase and its contents and told her of Alex's discoveries, their enquiries and the latest developments. Like Hetty and Lottie, she was very moved by the postcard sent by Peter.

"I see this was posted on January 2nd 1942 and now you tell me he died on February 7th that same year. So sad. Little did the poor man realise when he wrote it that he had just a whisker more than a month to live. I find that terribly upsetting."

Lottie sighed as Grace handed back the card. "Yes, we feel the same way and I think it's probably because of the obvious closeness of the twin brothers that we're so determined to find out what happened to David."

"Well let's hope you can track down this Simon Berryman and he can answer some of your questions."

"Fingers crossed," said Hetty, "but it's a pity we can't go down to the charity shop today. Still never mind we'll go tomorrow."

"Why can't you go down today?" Grace seemed eager for the sisters to discover more.

Hetty tutted. "Because it's Sunday, Grace, and so they're closed."

"Is it? Oh, silly me. Being away from home and not having a routine I don't know what day it is."

"Anyway, I think our brains have had quite enough names and dates to cope with for one day." Hetty put David's things back in the suitcase and closed the lid.

Grace smiled sweetly. "I can understand you getting muddled with names because I've contemplated looking into my family history since Mum went but it looks too confusing and I don't think I'd get very far."

"Why not?" Hetty asked.

"Well, I might be alright on Dad's side because Dunkerley is hardly a common name but my mother was a Smith, Anne Smith would you believe, so I can't see getting very far with that."

"Hetty chuckled. "Yes, I see your point."

"Anyway, what about the pond? Have you decided where to have it yet?"

"No we haven't." said Lottie. "We've discussed it but got no further than that. Perhaps we could sort it out now."

Hetty stood up. "Yes, no time like the present."

"Where would you put it if it were your project?" Hetty asked Grace, as they walked through the kitchen and out into the back garden.

"Well, it needs to be away from trees to avoid leaf fall in autumn and if you want to attract things like dragonflies it will need to be in full sun because they like to be warm."

"I know the feeling," said Hetty.

Grace laughed. "And another thing, ideally ponds look best when in the lowest part of the garden but as your garden is pretty level that's not possible."

They wandered around and finally decided on a patch where no flowers grew and the area was a mass of weeds.

"I should imagine this at one time was a vegetable plot," reasoned Grace, "seeing that nothing cultivated is growing here."

Lottie nodded. "Yes and that's why we've not bothered with this area because we did think of having vegetables here too but to be honest neither of us could raise the energy to dig it over and so a pond is a much better idea. Don't you agree, Het?"

"Absolutely, we want the garden to be as low maintenance as possible because we're neither of us getting any younger."

"Are you planning the pond?" called a voice from behind. They all turned to see Zac approaching.

"Yes, and we're having it here." Lottie pointed to the overgrown mass of weeds.

"Cool," said Zac, "it'll look great there and I'll be able to see it from my bedroom window when I get back in there."

"Sounds like we'd better get on with it then," laughed Lottie, "so that you can see it finished before you go home."

"Well now you need to decide what shape you want it and how big," said Grace, as she walked around the mass of weeds, "and then you can mark it out."

"There are some old tins of spray paint on top of the old table in the garage." Lottie revealed. "They were here when we moved in but I don't know whether or not they have any paint in them."

"Ideal if they have," said Grace.

"I'll go and check," Zac turned towards the garage.

"Just a minute. Before you go, Zac. Do you ladies have a strimmer?" Grace asked, "Because it would be much easier to mark out and dig if the weeds were chopped down."

"We do," Lottie answered promptly, "It's also in the garage."

"I'll get it and I'll see if there's any paint still in the tins as well," said Zac.

"The strimmer's hanging on the wall behind the door," Lottie called after him.

"Let's bring the bench that's in the front garden round here," suggested Hetty, "it'll be somewhere to sit then while the pond's being done and afterwards too of course."

"Good idea."

As Hetty and Lottie arrived with the bench and searched for a level spot on which to place it, Zac emerged from the garage.

"Why's there an old carpet in there?" he asked, as he laid down the strimmer and a rake and shook a near full can of paint.

"Oh that: it's from your room," said Lottie, "but we've not got round to taking it to the dump yet."

"An old carpet. Ideal," enthused Grace, "You can use that to line the pond before you put the liner in."

Hetty frowned. "Why would we do that?"

"To stop any stones left in the earth from puncturing the liner."

"Oh, I see, what a good idea."

"Shall I do the strimming?" Zac asked.

"Please do," said Hetty, as she sat down on the bench where she was joined by Lottie and Grace.

After the weeds were cut down, Zac raked them up and carried them to the compost heap at the bottom of the garden.

"So what shape do you want the pond to be?" he asked as he picked up the tin of paint.

"I think ovalish," said Lottie, "Do you ladies agree?"

"Definitely," they replied in unison.

Zac then slowly marked out the shape as instructed by the three ladies.

In the evening, Hetty, Lottie and Zac went to the Crown and Anchor for a meal. As they neared an empty table, Hetty pointed out a notice pinned to the French doors which led out to the sun terrace; it was about a raft race.

"Sounds fun," she said, as she pulled out a chair from beneath the table.

Lottie nodded. "As long as the weather's good."

Zac laid his phone on the table before he sat. "Fingers crossed it will be. It's only the second year the village has had one. Emma and Kyle were telling me about it the other day. Apparently they're in the process of making a raft so they can enter."

Hetty looked puzzled. "How come we didn't see it last year then? I mean we were here on holiday in August, weren't we?"

"Because they had it at Easter last year but decided to go for August this year because there will be more people around."

"I see."

"So what sort of raft are your friends making?" Lottie asked.

"I don't really know because I've not seen it yet but they're going to be dressed as pirates. They've asked me to join them and so I probably shall."

"How exciting," said Hetty, as she picked up the menu, "if you do take part we shall definitely come and watch it."

"Well, I think I'd like to see it whether Zac's in it or not," chuckled Lottie, "It should be very entertaining if the rafts are all homemade."

"Which they have to be," Zac stated, emphatically. "It's in the rules of entry."

Chapter Seven

On Monday morning Hetty and Lottie took out their sun hats from the cupboard underneath the stairs ready to wear for a visit to the charity shop. Before they left they took mugs of coffee up to the workers in the loft and told them they'd be away for an hour or so but if they needed anything Zac was out in the back garden with Emma making a start to the pond.

"Any luck with your investigations?" Basil asked, as he nodded towards the area in the attic where the suitcase was found.

"Yes, we've made a little headway," Hetty responded, "and that's why we're off out. We're going down to the charity shop to ask Maisie and Daisy if they know anything about a family called Berryman and a Simon Berryman in particular. We've learned that the Berrymans used to live in the village, you see, and through marriage they were related to the Tregears."

"Not only did they live in this village," Lottie added, "they lived in this house."

Hetty nodded. "That's right, they did."

"Perhaps they're the folks that had skeletons in their closets," chuckled Sid.

"Shush Sid," urged Hetty, "Lottie and I have agreed to forget about that silly Scrabble game. Anyway, I'm sure it meant nothing."

"What's a closet?" Mark asked.

"A cupboard," chuckled Basil.

"Or closet can also mean someone is doing something secretly," lectured Lottie, "A closet smoker for instance would be someone who smoked but claimed they didn't."

Mark frowned. Hetty patted his shoulder and then turned to her sister.

"Don't confuse the lad, Lottie."

"Sorry, Mark. Ignore me I'm inclined to waffle."

"So what makes you think the old dears in the charity shop will know anything about the Berrymans?" Basil asked.

"Because according to Kitty one of them has a brother who was friends with a young Berryman who lived here."

"I see."

"Berryman, not heard that name before," said Mark, as he took a packet of nails from the toolbox, "and I've lived here all my life."

Basil gave Mark a friendly poke. "You mean all nineteen years of it."

"Yeah, okay, not long I suppose." He grinned, "I wish you'd tell me how old you are, Baz."

"I'm as old as my tongue but older than my teeth."

Hetty laughed. "I had an aunt who always said that when I tried to find out her age."

In the corner Sid stooped to measure a piece of copper pipe for the shower room radiator. "So what did these Berrymans do?"

"They were undertakers," Lottie calmly stated.

Sid fell backwards, laughing.

Hetty frowned. "What's so funny?"

"Berryman," chuckled Sid, wiping tears from his eyes, "what an appropriate name for an undertaker."

Grace Dunkerley, enthused by the idea of seeing dragonflies, took a mug of coffee which she had made in her guest room out into the garden of Tuzzy-Muzzy and sat down on a wooden bench which overlooked the well-established pond. While she was there, a man in his late-forties came out and stood on the opposite side.

"Any fish in here do you know?"

"Yes, I'm told there are Koi Carp," disclosed Grace, "I've certainly seen movement amongst the water lilies but sadly as yet no fish."

"Koi Carp, in that case I shall sit here and hope to see one or two." He sat down on the path which ran round the pond.

"I've not seen you before," commented Grace, "have you only just arrived?"

The man nodded. "Yes, we got here last night. We being the wife and I."

"Oh, I didn't see you at breakfast but then I was the first down so must have missed you."

"You would have because we were the last. In fact we only just made it."

Grace smiled. "Well had you been late I'm sure Chloe wouldn't have turned you away."

"That's good to hear." He sprang to his feet and walked round to Grace and held out his hand. "My name's Malcolm, Malcolm Jackson."

Grace shook his hand. "Grace Dunkerley," she said.

"May I?" he asked, pointing to the empty space on the bench.

"Be my guest," Grace moved along so that he had plenty of room.

Malcolm sat down. "Lovely spot this, I'm so glad we found it on our internet search. We knew we wanted to come to Cornwall but didn't have any idea where as neither of us had ever been here before. I must admit it's even better than we expected."

"Cornwall or the guesthouse?"

"Both, not that we've seen much of Cornwall yet."

"You'll love it especially if the weather is kind. And there are all sorts of interesting places to visit. Not that I've been around much yet."

"Yes, we thought we'd go over to that Saint Michael's Mount place this morning. It looks rather intriguing and I should imagine in the moonlight it could double up for Count Dracula's castle."

Grace laughed. "Yes I daresay it could."

Malcolm looked at his watch and tutted. "Dear, dear, she said she'd only be ten minutes. The wife that is. She's gone up to our room to change and put some make-up on and she's already been gone half an hour."

Grace smiled. "But there's no rush, you're on holiday so have all the time in the world."

"True, but I'm a school teacher and so I'm used to working by the clock."

"A teacher, eh, so what's your subject?"

"History and I love it. That's one of the reasons I want to go to the Mount and of course and any other historic places while we're here."

"Does your wife teach?"

Malcom shook his head. "No but she is at the same school as me. She's the school secretary."

"That's convenient. For travel I mean."

"Yes, it is."

"And do you have children?"

"Two girls, both in their teens. Seventeen and nineteen. They're currently on holiday in Ibiza but I don't want to dwell on that fact."

"Hmm, I sympathise."

"How about you. Any children?"

"No, I've never been the maternal kind."

Malcolm nodded. "Yes, we're all different and have different aspirations, I suppose."

"I've got to know the two ladies who live next door," Grace pointed towards Primrose Cottage where the roof was just visible over the top of a camellia. "They discovered an old suitcase hidden beneath floorboards in their loft recently. Its contents should interest you. They appear to have belonged to someone who disappeared during the Second World War. They're trying to find out something about him so that would be right up your street."

"Really. Now that does sound interesting. Perhaps you could introduce me to them sometime."

"Ah, there you are," said an elegantly dressed woman with not a hair out of place as she appeared from the other side of flowering shrubs, "I'm ready now."

Malcolm stood up. "Good, but before we go, Belinda, let me introduce you to Grace. She's also a guest here."

Belinda held out her hand. "Pleased to meet you, Grace."

"Likewise." After the handshake, Grace quickly hid her hands behind her back conscious of the contrast between her own short clipped nails and Belinda's immaculate talons, which she deemed worthy of a place on an advertisement board for nail polish.

The visit to the charity shop proved fruitful. It was Daisy whose brother was friends with Simon Berryman and after hearing about the suitcase, Daisy rang him on her mobile to see if he knew where Simon was now. To the delight of Hetty and Lottie he was still in Cornwall and living on the outskirts of Truro. Daisy's brother was even able to provide a telephone number and an address.

Afterwards Hetty and Lottie walked along Pentrillick's main street, busy with holidaymakers sauntering along the pavements in small groups, laughing, chatting and seemingly enjoying the pleasant spell of good weather.

"Funny seeing people walking through the village in swimwear and skimpy summer clothing, isn't it, Het? I mean, people wouldn't walk around half dressed back home in Northants but it's quite the norm here."

Hetty laughed. "Yes, I see what you mean and I must admit I do notice it this year whereas last summer when we were holidaymakers ourselves I thought nothing of it."

"Precisely. Anyway, shall we pop in for a coffee?" Lottie asked as they approached Taffeta's Tea Shoppe, "then we can mull over what we've learned today and decide what our next move should be."

Hetty agreed. "Yes, I must admit seeing inside Taffeta's place always cheers me up."

"Oh dear, I didn't know you were feeling miserable." They stopped by the Tea Shoppe window.

"I'm not, it's just a figure of speech."

The café had been refurbished since Taffeta had taken over the business earlier in the year. Gone were Chloe's floral curtains and the bright yellow paint on the walls. Three walls were now pink and the fourth was papered with multi-coloured bows in all shapes and sizes on a white background. The curtains were in a fabric of the same design as the wallpaper as were the tablecloths. Only the floor was unchanged.

Taffeta dressed much like her décor. She had long blonde hair, tied back in a ponytail held together in a large taffeta bow. She wore a black knee length skirt part covered with a frilly white apron, and a chiffon blouse fastened at the neck with a large taffeta bow. The colours of her blouses varied from day to day and always matched the bow in her hair.

No-one knew much about Taffeta but many doubted it was her real name. All that was known was that she was in her late twenties, was married to Anthony Pascoe, a local lad from

Penzance and the couple had met two years previously when Taffeta was on holiday in Cornwall and that they had married soon after. They bought the café because Taffeta had always fancied having her own business, and they lived in the flat over the tea rooms. Anthony was a financial advisor with an office in Penzance and was red-hot at cricket.

But whether or not the locals liked Taffeta's ribbons and bows all agreed that she had a warm personality, worked hard and ran the business efficiently. She employed two part-time staff: Tess Dobson, who lived in the village and had done so for many years, and Daisy's granddaughter, Tulip.

After leaving the café Hetty and Lottie walked down to the beach where they bought ice creams and sat on one of the benches to eat them. The tide was low and several people were in the sea. On the water's edge children paddled and jumped in and out of the waves, laughing and giggling if the water splashed their faces. Much of the sand and shingle was taken with sunbathers, children building sandcastles and picnickers eating food from wicker baskets or takeaway fish and chips; while out at sea, Bernie the Boatman was chugging away from the shore with half a dozen anglers in his boat.

"It'll soon be a year since we first set foot in this village as holidaymakers," said Hetty, "What a lot of water has gone under the bridge since then."

Lottie smiled. "And who'd have thought on that first day that we'd end up living here. Strange how things work out."

"Isn't it just."

In the back garden of Primrose Cottage, Zac and Emma were busy digging a hole for the pond. The earth they removed they tossed onto a heap to be spread around the garden when the job was finished.

"Keep up the good work," shouted a familiar voice.

Zac looked round to see Sid approaching along with Basil and Mark. All were carrying lunch boxes.

"Do you mind if we come and watch you while we eat our lunches?" Sid chuckled as he sat down on a garden bench.

"You can give us a hand if you like," suggested Zac, wiping his sweaty forehead on the back of his hand.

"I might just do that," said Sid, removing clingfilm from his sandwiches, "you both look a bit hot and flustered."

"We feel it too," sighed Emma, laying down her spade and straightening her back, "I think we ought to have a break, Zac."

"Okay, you sit down and I'll go and make us all a mug of tea."

"No, no, I'll do it," Emma stepped out from the hole, "It'll be nice to get indoors and out of the sun."

Zac sat down on the grass, removed his shoes and tipped out soil from each one.

"Found anything interesting?" Basil asked, as he sat down beside Sid.

Zac grinned. "A button, several pieces of broken china and an old coin but I can't quite make out what it is."

Basil held out his hand. "Chuck it here."

Zac threw the coin which Basil caught and turned over in his hand. "Ah, it's an old farthing. They ceased to be legal tender in the year I was born."

"When was that then?" Mark asked, legs crossed as he sat on the grass near to Zac.

"1960."

Mark chuckled and wagged his fingers. "So you're fifty seven. I knew you'd let it slip one day."

Emma brought out mugs of tea on a tray and placed it down on the grass. She then sat down near to Mark who was closing up his lunch box having gobbled down his sandwiches and chocolate bars.

"Can I do some digging?" he eagerly asked, as he took a sip of his tea, "I rather fancy digging for treasure."

"Be our guest," grinned Zac, "but if what we've found so far is anything to go by I don't think there's much chance of finding treasure."

"Thanks," Mark sprang to his feet and jumped into the hole.

"If you dig the hole deep enough you can put the old plaster from your ceiling in the bottom," suggested Basil, "It'd be one way of getting rid of it."

Sid agreed. "You'll need to break it up though, but a good stamping on it when it's in place should do the trick."

"That's a good idea," said Zac, "I'll see what the ladies think when they get back."

After digging for ten minutes, Mark struck something solid and excitedly dug away the earth to see what he had found. To his dismay it was an old rusty knife. In distain he tossed it aside. Sid picked it up.

"It's a kitchen knife and would have been a beauty in its day. Look it has a bone handle." He showed it to Basil who brushed away some earth to reveal Sheffield just legible on the blade.

"Someone must have been really fed up when they lost that," tutted Basil.

Sid polished the handle on the sleeve of his shirt. "Someone must have been really careless as well. I mean, surely something of this size wouldn't be easy to lose."

"I dunno," said Basil, "I've lost garden tools before now and thought I'd never see them again and then they've turned up a few years later when I've been digging over the garden or transplanting things. In fact I lost my mum's favourite trowel once when I were a lad and she was not best pleased."

When Lottie and Hetty arrived back at Primrose Cottage they were astounded to find Zac and Emma had almost finished digging out the pond.

"Just the marginal shelf to do that Grace said about," stated Zac, "unless you want the pond any deeper. Although we've already gone down deeper than you said because Basil suggested putting the old ceiling rubble in the bottom to get rid of it."

Lottie glanced at the unsightly heap of old plaster. "Oh, well done, Basil: that's an excellent idea. We were wondering what to do with it. I must compliment him when I next see him."

"Anyway, it looks fine to me," agreed Hetty, "but we'll ask Grace what she thinks when we next see her."

"Talk of the devil," laughed Lottie, as Grace walked round the side of the house, waving. "Is it alright if I join you?" she called.

"Of course, of course. Come and tell us what you think," gushed Hetty, "Do you think they've dug deep enough?"

"Oh yes," said Grace, as she reached the side of hole, "you must have been working flat out to get all this done in one morning."

"We did have a bit of help," confessed Emma, "Mark was keen to find treasure and so did a bit of digging during his lunch break."

"Treasure," chortled Hetty.

"Yes, he didn't find any of course although he did find this." Zac picked up the knife from the grass where it lay and passed it to his great aunt.

"Oh dear, what a shame," tutted Hetty, "that would have been a beauty in its day."

Zac laughed. "That's just what Sid said."

"Great minds," reflected Hetty. She handed the knife to Lottie and then sat down on the bench.

"Any news about the chap who used to live here? I can't remember his name." Grace asked as she sat down beside Hetty.

"Simon Berryman, and yes, we've got his phone number and his address. It was Daisy from the charity shop whose brother was friends with Simon."

"And still is," Lottie added.

"Well done you. So is he still living in Cornwall?"

"Yes, in Truro so hopefully we'll be able to visit him quite soon."

"Good work, ladies," Grace enthused, "and I met someone of interest today too. Staying next door is a chap called Malcolm Jackson. He teaches history and sounded quite enthusiastic when I told him about the suitcase, so he could be useful in your search for David Tregear as well."

"That's interesting," agreed Hetty, "and is he also on his own?"

"Oh no, he has a stunning wife called Belinda whose hands tell me she's never done a physical day's work in her life."

On Tuesday morning Zac went down to the village to help Kyle and a few others put the finishing touches to their raft and to discuss ideas for costumes before Kyle went to work at the Crown and Anchor at eleven thirty.

Just before midday, Zac arrived back at Primrose Cottage and began to shovel the old plaster into the bottom of the pond. Hetty and Lottie offered to help him but he insisted on doing it himself.

"No Emma this afternoon?" Lottie asked.

"No, she's gone shopping with her mum. They're going round the charity shops in Penzance looking for things we can use for our pirate costumes. They asked me if I wanted to go as well but I said no because I wanted to get this done while the weather's good."

Lottie looked to the blue sky. "Very wise. It's lovely at the moment but we all know it can change at the drop of a hat."

Zac laughed. "You do say some funny things, Gran."

"Funny things." Lottie was puzzled.

"Yes, you said the weather could change at the drop of a hat. Why a drop of a hat?"

Lottie shrugged her shoulders. "I've absolutely no idea."

Hetty standing nearby dead-heading her favourite dahlia, took out her phone from her pocket and Googled it. "Apparently it comes from the American West where the signal for a fight was often just the drop of a hat."

"Well I never," chortled Lottie, "You learn something new every day."

Zac cupped his left hand behind his ear. "Is that a lorry I can hear?"

"Hmm, sounds like it," Hetty agreed, "I'd better go and see. It might be building stuff for the chaps."

To her delight it was the builders' merchants with a delivery of plasterboard sheets and so once it was unloaded and carried indoors, Basil and Mark abandoned the attic, carried it upstairs and began to put up a new ceiling in Zac's room.

Chapter Eight

On Wednesday morning, Hetty and Lottie, delighted with the progress being made in the attic, Zac's bedroom and with the pond, contemplated how best to spend their day. After toying with several ideas, they agreed that since both were eager to track down any Berrymans with connections to Pentrillick that a trip to Truro was their best option in order to look up Simon Berryman. However, they decided not to phone in advance to check that he was in because by doing so they would have to explain who they were and why they wanted to meet him and it was agreed best to do that in person rather than over the phone.

Hetty drove because Lottie insisted as she'd never driven to Truro before she would most likely get lost, even though Hetty assured her that was unlikely to happen as the route was clearly sign-posted.

They found the house with ease and parked a few doors away on the opposite side of the road in order to weigh up the neighbourhood. The area was well kept, gardens were tidy and there was not a hint of graffiti anywhere. After walking a short distance along the slabbed pavement, they opened the Berrymans' garden gate, stepped onto the path and then Lottie feeling a little tense, knocked on the door. After what seemed like several minutes but was in fact only fifty seconds, a man in his sixties with thick white hair answered.

"Mr Berryman," gushed Lottie, nervously, "Mr Simon Berryman?"

The man frowned. "Yes and what can I do for you, ladies?"

"We'd like to ask you some questions about your family history," gabbled Lottie, "You see, we found some things that relate to your ancestors. The Berryman side of your family, that is and we're pretty sure you will be interested to hear what we have to say."

"Really, that sounds fascinating, you'd better come in then." He opened the door wide and they went inside.

"This is my wife, Sheila," he announced, as he led them into the living room where a lady sat crocheting by the window. "Sheila, these ladies are here because apparently they've some information about Berrymans from years gone by."

"And some questions to ask," Hetty calmly added.

Sheila put down her handiwork. "Sounds interesting. Would you like a cup of tea?"

Hetty and Lottie both nodded. "That would be lovely, thank you," said Lottie, "both white, no sugar."

"Okay, please sit down and I'll be back in a jiffy."

"Better wait for Sheila before you tell me your news," suggested Simon, who himself sat once the sisters were seated, "she's so much better at retaining facts than I am but you can at least tell me how you found out where I lived."

"Through Daisy," Hetty divulged, "and I've just realised that we've known her for a year now but I don't know her surname. Anyway, she lives in Pentrillick and works in the charity shop there. Apparently you're a friend of her brother."

"Oh yes, that'll be Clive, he has a sister called Daisy," Simon laughed, "Clive and I have known each other for longer than I care to remember."

When Sheila returned with mugs of tea and a plate of biscuits, Hetty and Lottie in turn told of the discovery of the suitcase in the attic and the results of their neighbour's delving into the family history of the Tregears and how the Tregears were related through marriage to the Berrymans.

"Good heavens," muttered Simon as the news sank in, "I must pay you a visit and have a look at that suitcase and its contents, if that's alright."

"Of course," exclaimed Hetty, "we'd be delighted to show you. I'll give you our address before we leave."

Simon chuckled. "But I already know it. You said you live at Primrose Cottage. Well, that's where I was born."

Hetty tutted. "Yes, of course. Kitty told us you lived there when she was young and you used to walk to school together."

"Kitty, what Kitty Vickery?"

"Yes, only she's Kitty Thomas now."

"So she did marry. Last I heard she was living on her own in the house her family have owned for years."

"She married earlier this year and her husband is a very nice man called Tommy." Hetty put down her tea and took a biscuit from the plate.

"Well, I look forward to seeing her again," chuckled Simon, "we were quite good friends when we were little."

Hetty smiled. "So we've heard."

"Right, so what do you want me to tell you?"

"Well, I suppose anything you can remember about living at Primrose Cottage would be a good place to start," said Lottie, feeling it was time that she got in on the conversation.

Simon nodded. "Okay, well my dad was called George and obviously was a Berryman and he bought Primrose Cottage in 1939 just before the war broke out. Harold, his father, gave him a nice wad of money for the deposit and if I remember correctly, Dad told me his sister, my Aunt Polly, looked after the house for him until 1948 when he married my mother." Simon paused to take a sip of tea.

"So until 1948 your father lived at Primrose Cottage alone?" Hetty surmised.

"Yes, yes, no actually no, I don't think he did. I vaguely remember Dad saying something about a chap who drove the hearse lodging there during the war. He avoided conscription because he worked on one of the farms and was also a volunteer for the lifeboat. I can't remember his name though. But then I probably never knew it and it might only have been for a few months anyway."

"Never mind, I don't expect it matters," said Hetty.

"Unless it was Jimmy," suggested Lottie, "Remember the postcard, Het. Peter said he hoped old Jimmy was behaving."

"Good point," Hetty agreed, "Does the name Jimmy sound at all familiar, Simon?"

"Well, I can't say that it does. Jimmy," he mused, "no it doesn't ring a bell." He closed his eyes, "I'm trying to recall if Mum ever mentioned him, because she and Dad were together for some time before they married so she must have known him. Well, they'd actually known each other since they were kids. Mum was called Betty, by the way, but sadly I don't remember a great deal about her. She died when I was six years old. Well I was nearly seven. In fact it was a week before my seventh birthday. It was very sad. Poor Mum must have tripped on a loose bit of carpet on the landing or something like that because she fell down the stairs and broke her neck. No-one was in the house at the time so she wasn't found for a while. I was at school, you see, and Dad was at work and I suppose the lodger chap was as well. Damn, I wish I had some inkling as to what his name was."

"Yes, we're really sorry about what happened to your mother," sympathised Lottie, "Kitty told us what little she remembered and how sad it was. It must be dreadful to lose a parent especially at such a young age."

Simon nodded. "Yes, it was but Dad was brilliant and so I never felt neglected or anything like that."

"So can you tell us anything about your father's stepbrothers, the twins, Peter and David Tregear? Peter obviously died before you were born but what about David? Have you any idea what happened to him?"

Simon shook his head. "No not really. I asked Dad about him once because Grandma Florence who was actually my step-grandmother had a picture of David and Peter on the mantel piece in her room at the hotel. They were a nice looking couple of lads but they weren't identical like some twins are. He said that no-one knew where David was but it's thought he might have run away because he was afraid of being called-up to go to war and of course having already lost his brother that would have made him afraid, I suppose."

"If that's the case," said Lottie, "David was definitely still alive in 1942 when Peter died but it seems a little odd that David didn't attend his brother, Peter's funeral."

"Is that right?" Simon asked, "I mean, how do you know that?"

"Because our next door neighbour, Alex, looked at a local newspaper article about the funeral on-line and he wasn't listed amongst the mourners."

"Hmm, very odd."

"Yet the brothers must have been close because Peter sent David a postcard in January 1942 which was a month before he died."

Simon appeared to be nonplussed. "In which case if David was still in Pentrillick when Peter died he must have disappeared soon after."

"Very soon after," said Lottie, "If he didn't attend the funeral because he'd run away."

Simon shook his head. "Actually, I very much doubt that that was the case because train drivers were exempt from conscription and he was also crew on the local lifeboat, same as the lodger chap."

"How about your father?" Hetty asked, "What did he do during the war?"

"Dad stayed at home and ran the family business. He couldn't go to war, you see, because he was medically unfit. Poor chap suffered from asthma and had flat feet."

"Oh dear," sympathised Lottie, "I take it he didn't serve on the lifeboat either then."

"No, but I always got the impression he wished he could have. The Pentrillick lifeboat was quite a big thing once upon a time but it must have shut down either before or soon after I was born because I can't remember there ever having been one when I was a boy."

"So was Peter ever crew on the lifeboat?" asked Hetty.

Simon shook his head. "No, because apparently he was afraid of the water and had a fear of drowning but I don't know why."

Lottie smiled. "Well, I can understand that. It'd take a strong stomach to be out on choppy waters and I know my poor old tum couldn't take it."

Hetty frowned as she tried to make sense of information received. "Now what you've told us, Simon, is really interesting, because if it's highly unlikely that David would ever have been called up because of his occupation, then the running away story was either pure fabrication or just a wild guess by someone."

"Hmm, I must admit it's starting to look that way," Simon conceded, "The fact he'd have been exempt from conscription never occurred to me before. But then when I first heard about David I was only a kid so I took what was told to me as fact."

"By why?" Hetty was confused," Why would someone make it up?"

"No idea," said Simon. "It makes no sense at all."

"It's just struck me," blurted Lottie, "Would the lifeboat you've mentioned be the one whose house is along the coast and has now been converted into a studio?"

"Yes, the very one. It's not been a lifeboat house for some time now but as I said I can't remember exactly when it closed, not that it matters. Not as regards the family history anyway."

"I've just remembered something," said Lottie, as she reached for her handbag. From it she took a brown envelope containing the picture that was in the suitcase. She handed it to Simon. "I know you've seen a picture of David and Peter before, albeit a long time ago, but you'd still probably like to see this."

Simon opened the envelope. "Ah, this must have been taken around the same time as the one Grandma Florence had because I recognise the twins instantly. And the boat, Goliath I remember being told that was David's fishing boat. Fishing was his passion and he'd be out at sea whenever he had the time. I wonder what happened to the boat."

"Yes, you saying that has reminded me that's something else we must look into as well," said Hetty.

Simon handed the photograph to his wife. "You're a clever woman, Sheila. What do you make of all this?"

"Well, I've never heard about these members of your family before but looking at it as an outsider I'd agree that it seems highly unlikely that David would have run away without just cause and if he had he most certainly wouldn't have left behind his identity card and personal possessions. I mean, surely back during the war you'd have been in real trouble if you couldn't show an identity card if asked."

Simon nodded. "Yes I daresay you're right. I've never had reason to question any of it before but in the light of the suitcase's discovery, I'd certainly like to know what really did happen now."

"What can you tell us about your grandfather, Harold Berryman? We know he was a widower and married the twins' mother, Florence Tregear who was a widow and owned the Pentrillick Hotel. Did you know him at all?"

"Oh yes and he was lovely. Funny, generous and a fantastic mimic. He taught me to play cricket and used to take me river fishing. In retrospect I think he wanted to try and make up for the fact I'd lost my mother. I often stayed at the hotel with him and Grandma Florence. I suppose it also helped Dad out. Dad had the business to look after, you see. As you already know he was an undertaker." Simon laughed. "Used to get my leg pulled at school for that. Funny though but death isn't something I've ever feared and that must be because I thought nothing of seeing coffins and suchlike. I mean, to me the hearse was like a tractor must be to a farmer's son."

"So did your grandfather Harold not work at the undertakers when he got older?" Lottie asked.

"Occasionally he did but most of the work was done by Dad and Aunt Polly. Granddad helped out if they were really busy and I suppose he did more during the war but I think he preferred to help at the hotel. He'd worked at the funeral parlour since he were a teenager, you see, and then when he was twenty five he took over most of the responsibility from his father who suffered from poor health. It was his father who started the business but I couldn't tell you when that was or even what he was called. Not that it matters. I think Granddad was glad to do something different. He liked to do the hotel gardens. I remember helping him, as a boy. I got to know the names of flowers through him. Wild and cultivated. He taught me the names of birds too and lots of other wild creatures that live around here. He was a real countryman at heart."

"And what about your father's sister, Polly? What happened to her?"

Simon shrugged his shoulders. "I don't really know. As I just said, all I remember is her helping at the undertaking business and she helped at the hotel too but then she moved away. I don't know why but she probably wanted to do something a little more interesting. I don't really remember her much because she left when I was quite young. I can't remember when exactly but I was still at primary school. I liked Aunt Polly though, she had a lovely smile and used to make cakes. She read me stories too. I've often thought it'd be nice to trace her but it'd be impossible if she married which I hope she did because she'd have made a great mum and housewife."

"Ouch," laughed Hetty, "not politically correct to say things like that in this day and age."

Simon smiled. "No, I suppose not."

"I'm beginning to get a picture now," said Hetty, "but sadly none of it solves the mystery as to where David went so I guess we'll never know."

"Out of curiosity, when did you and your father leave Primrose Cottage?" Lottie asked.

"Sometime in the nineteen sixties after Granddad died and that was in 1964. Grandma Florence was already dead, she died in 1961. Dad inherited the hotel and so sold the cottage and the hotel, closed up the undertaking business and we moved to Penzance. Needless to say we were quite wealthy then but Dad frittered most of it away because when he died ten years ago there was nothing much left apart from the house. Still, good luck to him. At least he enjoyed his premature retirement."

Hetty frowned. "But surely some of the money raised through the sales of the hotel and undertaking business should have gone to your Aunt Polly, her being your father's sister."

"Do you know I'd never thought of that before. Of course the money would have been shared with her as I expect Granddad left everything to them both in his will anyway. Thank you, Hetty, because now I understand why there was less in the coffers than I'd anticipated. It also means Dad didn't squander his inheritance after all."

"And it's probably why he sold everything," said Lottie, "so the money could be shared equally, that is."

"It also means that if your father shared the inheritance with his sister he must have known where she was in 1964 when your grandfather died," said Hetty.

Simon frowned. "Another good point and now you come to mention it I vaguely remember we used to get Christmas cards from her when I was young. But I don't remember any in later years."

"Probably took the money and went to live somewhere hot and sunny," said Lottie.

Simon nodded. "Yes, and who could blame her?"

"I wonder why your dad never remarried?" mused Sheila," after all he was only a young man."

"He would have been thirty nine when he lost Mum. I know he was greatly saddened by her death and perhaps he didn't think it right to replace her."

Hetty and Lottie each had a second cup of tea and then left soon after with Simon and Sheila promising to call very soon to see the suitcase and its contents.

When they arrived back in Pentrillick, the sisters went to the Crown and Anchor for a late lunch hoping to see Bernie the Boatman in order to ask if he recognised David's boat, Goliath, while they had the photograph with them. He wasn't in and so as soon as they had eaten they walked down to the beach. To their delight he was there chatting to some holidaymakers.

"Have you finished for the day?" Hetty asked.

"Yes, I only go out once a day as it can take several hours for my enthusiasts to catch any fish. I don't think I could face going out twice anyway and of course what time I go and come back is down to the tide."

Hetty nodded. "Yes, I suppose so although it's all gobbledegook to me. You know, ebbing, flooding, spring tides, neap tides and suchlike. To me it's just low or high water."

"Anyway," said Lottie, taking the brown envelope from her handbag, "what we're really here for is to see if you recognise this boat." She handed Bernie the photograph of Peter, David and the Goliath.

"Goliath," mused Bernie, scratching his head, "can't say that the name rings a bell, but it's definitely the beach here because there's the pub in the background. When do you reckon it was taken? It must be a few years back because it's before the pub's terrace was built and that was in the nineteen sixties."

"Sometime before 1942," answered Hetty, "because that's when Peter died and David went missing."

"Yes, that figures because there hasn't been any fishing in Pentrillick since the nineteen fifties. Not commercially anyway." He handed the photograph back to Lottie, "Nevertheless, I'll make a few enquiries and see if anyone knows what happened to the old girl."

"Girl," blurted Hetty, "surely Goliath is a chap's name."

Lottie tutted and looked heavenwards. "Oh, Het, all boats are referred to as *she*: even I know that."

When they arrived back in Blackberry Way, they found Grace leaning on the five bar gate of the field opposite their cottage. She waved as she saw them approaching.

"Hi, I called round to see you earlier but assumed you'd gone out because your car wasn't here. I didn't knock to find out though because I thought if Zac was out too then it's a fair way downstairs from the loft for the chaps to answer the door."

"We've been to Truro," gabbled Lottie, her voice tinged with excitement, "and Zac is in but he's in the back garden cutting the hedge. At least he was when we left."

"We've been to see Simon Berryman," explained Hetty, as she locked up the car, "You know, the chap we told you about who is friends with Daisy-from-the-charity-shop's brother. We hoped he'd be able to tell us a bit about the history of this place and the people who lived here."

"And did he?"

Hetty wrinkled her nose. "Yes, he did, and what he said helps a bit but on the whole I think we're probably even more muddled now than we were before."

"Without doubt," agreed Lottie. "My head's spinning."

"Nevertheless, do tell." Grace tilted her head to one side in anticipation.

"Of course. Come on, let's go inside and have a nice cuppa and a piece of cake."

As they approached the door, Grace nodded towards the feathery plumes swaying in front of the sitting room window. "That's a spectacular clump of pampas grass you have there."

"Do you like it?" Hetty asked. "It was already here when we moved in but I can't make my mind up as to whether I like it or not. It blocks out some of the light from the window, you see and it can look a bit messy."

Grace giggled. "Well I like it but I wouldn't grow it. Not in this day and age anyway."

"This day and age," Hetty repeated. "What do you mean?"

"I'm referring to the fact that it's very much out of favour right now and sales of it have plummeted." Grace laughed in a schoolgirl manner. "You're never going to believe why though."

Lottie and Hetty both stood with blank expressions on their faces.

"Well," Grace continued, "from what I've read its popularity has declined because it's now regarded as a secret signal to passers-by that its owners are happy to indulge in swinging."

"Indulge in swinging," Hetty was flabbergasted, "you're pulling my leg, Grace."

"I'm not, check it out and you'll find that a lot of nurseries have actually stopped stocking it simply because gardeners don't want it anymore."

"Hetty's been threatening to chop it down for some time," laughed Lottie, as she opened the front door, "I've always objected but I think you've changed my mind."

Once indoors they sat in the sitting room and while they drank tea, the sisters brought Grace up to date.

"So, what's this Simon Berryman like?" Grace asked.

"Really nice," said Hetty.

"And so is his wife," Lottie added.

"That's good to hear. I wonder if he has any pictures of his family."

Hetty nodded. "He has but sadly there aren't many and what there are aren't very good. Apparently a whole album of pictures got damaged when they were stored in a damp cupboard and so they had to be thrown away."

"Oh, that's sad," sighed Grace, "because old photos can't be replaced."

"Yes, and the ones that were unharmed weren't in the album because they were inferior," sighed Lottie, "Simon's going to look them out anyway and bring them when they come to see us."

"Excellent, I'm sure it will help if we can put faces to the names we have so far."

"Meanwhile, I think we must take another wander round the graveyard," Hetty suggested, "this time looking for Berrymans."

In the evening Simon Berryman phoned to say that he and Sheila had booked a room at Tuzzy-Muzzy for three nights on Friday, Saturday and Sunday. He said he thought the gods were on his side because the guest house had just minutes before had a cancellation because one of the two people due to stay in a double room had broken a leg.

"Brilliant," said Lottie, who had answered the phone, "we're really looking forward to your visit and no doubt we'll have come up with another list of questions by then."

"I look forward to trying to answer them," laughed Simon, "and I can't wait to see the house and village again."

Shortly after Simon's call, the phone rang again. Lottie answered it but there was no-one there. She cursed as she returned to the sitting room, sat down and picked up her knitting. Five minutes later it rang again. Lottie answered but as before there was no-one there. She slammed down the receiver. "Sodding nuisance calls, they really are a nuisance."

As Hetty laughed at the angry expression on her sister's face, the phone rang yet again.

"I'm not answering it," snapped Lottie, emphatically, picking up her knitting again and attacking it with vigour.

"All right, all right, keep your hair on." Hetty walked into the hallway and picked up the phone. There was no-one there. She dialled 1471 and was told the caller withheld their number.

"Perhaps it's a fault on the line," muttered Hetty, as she returned to the sitting room, "and for some reason it keeps making our phone ring."

But when she sat down and the phone rang again, she too felt angry. With a look of exasperation, Hetty entered the hallway and picked up the phone. "What the hell's going on," she bellowed down the receiver. She was shocked when her ear was met with heavy breathing. And then it stopped. There was a brief pause and then a piercing scream rang through the receiver. Hetty screamed also and dropped the phone onto the floor. When her heart stopped thumping loudly she picked it up. The line was clear and there were no more calls that night.

Chapter Nine

The following morning, Hetty and Lottie took the old carpet from the garage which had been in Zac's bedroom and carried it into the back garden ready to line the pond. Most of the plaster in the bottom of the hole had been broken into small pieces and Zac had sprinkled soil over it to fill in any gaps to make a smoother surface. With the aid of a sharp knife, the sisters cut the carpet into large strips and laid them over the plaster by slightly overlapping each one until the whole area was covered. To their delight there was just enough and nothing left over. When they returned indoors, Hetty ordered a pond liner from the supplier recommended to them by Chloe's brother, Alfie.

The sisters were in a good frame of mind despite the mysterious phone calls received the previous evening for they had concluded after a brief discussion that they must have been made by mischievous children who rang a number at random which just happened to be theirs.

In the afternoon, Hetty, who was sitting on the bottom tread of the stairs putting on her shoes to take Albert out for a walk, suggested Lottie come too and then they could wander around the churchyard to see if they could find any Berrymans. Lottie jumped at the idea and within ten minutes the three of them were walking down Long Lane towards the village.

They found several graves whose memorial stones told of Berrymans that predated the period they were interested in; they instantly disregarded them as they would not help with their investigations and walked on by. To their delight, a short distance away, they came across the graves of Harold Berryman and his second wife, Florence, who they knew to be mother of twins, Peter and David Tregear. A little further along they found the graves of Simon Berryman's parents, George Berryman and his wife, Betty whose death occurred in 1956 after a fall down the stairs.

Lottie tutted. "Poor Betty. Look, Het, she was only thirty four when she died."

"Yes, and I've just realised something. She died in our house."

"Oh dear, so she did. Primrose Cottage doesn't appear to have a very happy past, does it?"

"No, but perhaps we can change all that," Hetty suggested, "and we can turn it into a happy house."

"Well, it'll be happy for as long as Sid's there doing the plumbing. I've never known anyone so jovial."

"Absolutely. Anyway, we've seen all we set out to see here so we might as well go home now. Do you agree?"

As Lottie opened her mouth to reply something caught her eye. "Surely I'm mistaken. Look, Het. Look over there. Isn't that Peter's grave?"

Hetty frowned. "I'm not sure what you're getting at, Lottie. I mean, we know Peter's grave is over there. What of it?"

"Yes, but look what's on it. Follow me."

Hetty followed as Lottie marched across the grass to the final resting place of Peter Tregear. On his grave a dozen white roses graced the vase attached to the polished granite headstone.

"I've gone all goosepimply," whispered Lottie, rubbing her arms, "I mean, who can have put them there?" They weren't here the other day and there are no Tregears in the area now."

Hetty frowned. "Not that we know of. How peculiar. Perhaps then David really did run away and eventually married up-country somewhere. If so he may have had children and they or one of them are now living in the area having returned to their roots."

"Yes, could be, and he, she or they, put flowers on the grave of their Great Uncle Peter. But if that were the case then surely locals would know there were Tregears here again."

"Not if David had changed his name," reasoned Hetty.

"Or he might have kept his name but had a daughter who has now married and so changed her name."

"Or perhaps it was just a distant relative visiting."

Hetty cast her eyes all around the graveyard. "Well whatever the motive it means that someone in our midst has reason to remember him and I find it a little unnerving that we've absolutely no idea who that someone might be."

Simon and Sheila arrived at Tuzzy-Muzzy on Friday afternoon and as soon as they had unpacked their things they walked round to Primrose Cottage.

"Before we see the suitcase, may I have a look round?" Simon excitedly asked as Hetty held back the door and beckoned them to enter. "I'm itching to see the old place again."

"I can understand that," said Hetty, closing the door. "You'll be surprised when you get upstairs though because we're having the loft converted, so it'll look very different to how you remember it."

"Yes, you mentioned it the other day because that's how you found the suitcase."

Hetty tutted. "Of course. Silly me."

Simon found looking round the house brought back many memories and he gave a running commentary on how things used to be as he went from room to room. "I vaguely remember this being done," he cried, when he peeped inside the bathroom. "It was a bedroom before, you see. I must have been very young at the time, in fact no older than six, because I remember Mum being excited when it was finished and the thrill of having my first bath in here."

Inside Zac's room, Basil was plastering the new ceiling. "Oh my goodness. This was my room although it doesn't look as big as I remember. But I would've been much smaller then."

He crossed the landing and looked into Lottie's room. "This was Mum and Dad's room." He crossed to the window. "How well I remember that view. It's changed very little."

Hetty's bedroom, Simon recalled was the spare room in which Aunt Polly often slept.

At the top of the stairs he paused. "It must have been from here that Mum fell. I remember the carpet was frayed in places but of course it wasn't a lovely fitted carpet like you have now. It was just a long runner which ran along the middle of the bare floorboards."

After the tour of the house, Hetty made coffee while Lottie showed Simon and Sheila into the sitting room.

"I can't begin to tell you how much I appreciate you having invited me here," said Simon as he took a seat near to the window. "It's brought back so many memories. I feel quite emotional."

"And hopefully seeing the contents of the suitcase will bring back even more," said Hetty as she walked into the room with a tea tray, "although I realise the case goes back several years before you were born."

"When were you born?" Lottie asked, "I don't think we've established that yet."

"1949," Simon replied as Hetty handed him a mug of coffee.

"Ah, that makes you three years older than us then," calculated Lottie, "we were born in 1952."

"You're the same age as me then," said Sheila, nodding in the direction of the sisters, "I was born in that year too."

Hetty stood her coffee mug in the hearth and then left the room. She promptly returned with the suitcase which she laid at Simon's feet. "I'll leave you to look through it." She picked up her coffee and took a seat by the fireplace.

"There's also a pair of shoes and an overcoat," Lottie revealed, "they were in the loft alongside the case and we assume they were left out as there wasn't enough room for everything."

"And probably to spread the weight," reasoned Hetty, "as I'm sure if everything had been crammed in the case the ceiling would have come down long before now."

"Oh, and I've just remembered," Lottie sprang to her feet and picked up the old teddy bear from a stool in the corner of the room. "This little chap was also under the floorboards." She handed the bear to Simon. "The poor thing was stuffed in an old pillowslip."

"Goodness me," gasped Simon, as he turned the bear over in his hands, "this little fella would have belonged to David because I have one exactly the same. Grandma Florence gave him to me when I was a kid and asked me to take good care of him. He was very special, you see, because he used to belong to Peter. Apparently, her husband, Frank, bought Peter and David both identical bears for their third birthdays and the boys treasured them because they reminded them of their father who died soon after." Simon chuckled. "Peter's bear is called Gingerbread. He was named that by his father but I don't know why."

"If the bears were identical how did the boys know whose was whose?" Lottie asked.

"Good point and it must have been because of the tie. Peter's bear has a blue tie whereas this chap's is red."

"I see and do you by any chance know the name of this bear? Several of us have made suggestions such as Fred,

Pilchard, Saffron Bun and Old Jimmy but it'd be nice to know what David called him."

Simon chuckled. "Well, none of those names ring a bell but then I was probably never told his name. I'll put my thinking cap on later and see if a name springs to mind." He looked down at the suitcase. "Meanwhile, I think I'll have a look through this."

Simon sat the bear on the table and then knelt down on the floor. He lifted up the case lid and after shuffling through the contents he picked out the wooden boat. "Goliath, I'd forgotten all about Goliath until you showed me the photo the other day. This must have been carved by Peter Tregear because I remember going with Grandma Florence to put flowers on his grave and she told me that he was a carpenter before he went to war. In fact, I've just remembered, he worked at the undertakers too, making coffins I suppose."

"Ah, so that might be what brought the two families together," said Hetty.

"More than likely," Simon turned the boat over in his hands. "I'm really impressed with this. It's beautifully carved." He stood the boat on the table and a smile crossed his face. "Dad took me out in Goliath once but he said that he didn't have sea legs like the fishermen. Probably something to do with his flat feet." He looked at the sisters, "Have you had any luck finding out what happened to her? She can't be far away because if David went missing in 1942 it must still have been around in the fifties for me to remember it." He groaned. "What am I talking about? The fifties were sixty plus years ago so the boat might be long gone."

Hetty chuckled. "It's easy to lose track of time. Lottie and I are past masters at it. As for the boat, we've asked a friend of ours who does fishing trips in the village to investigate. Hopefully he'll be able to come up with something."

Simon frowned. "It's funny but a strange fuzzy memory is coming back. I was in the hallway here playing with a model car. Mum and Dad were in here talking and when I heard mention of David and Goliath my ears pricked up but their conversation didn't make sense. You see, Mum said something about David being dead and I was confused because I knew through teachings at Sunday school that David slew Goliath the giant with his sling and so he didn't die. Of course I realise now they weren't discussing a Bible story at all but must have been talking about David and his boat, Goliath." He chuckled. "And I suppose I must have got my wires crossed somehow and the death they referred to must have been Peter and not David. After all I was very young."

"And Peter died seven years before you were born anyway," said Sheila, working out in her head details of the Tregear/Berryman family tree, "so you wouldn't have known him at all."

"Absolutely," Simon agreed, "and as Mum died just before my seventh birthday I must have been very young when I overheard them talking."

Lottie nodded. "Yes, it's very easy to get childhood memories muddled. I used to think I could remember war planes flying overhead as a youngster but of course I couldn't have because I wasn't born until seven years after the war ended. My memory was no doubt confused by the many black and white war films that were on the television back in those days."

"Ah, those were the days," chuckled Simon, "black and white television and all of two channels. Although I actually remember when there was only one channel."

Hetty groaned. "So do I but let's not dwell on that fact as it makes me feel really old."

"Is your father still with us?" Lottie asked, calculating there was a slim possibility George Berryman might still be alive.

"Sadly not. He died in 2007 when he was ninety years old and although he was living in Penzance at the time we had him buried here in Pentrillick alongside Mum because that was his wish."

Hetty tutted. "You know Simon's father is no longer with us, Lottie. Remember, we saw his grave yesterday."

Lottie's face reddened. "Oh yes, silly me."

Simon smiled. "Don't worry, I'm finding it hard to keep track and I'm familiar with some of the names so it must be a really confusing for you."

"And as we established the other day, your father never remarried," commented Hetty.

"That's right and in a funny sort of way I'm glad he didn't because I don't think I would have liked to have a step-mother."

Sheila smiled. "Your father had a step-mother and from what I've gathered Florence was very nice."

"Yes, she was."

Lottie having recovered her embarrassment said: "I was just thinking. Whereabouts in the village was the undertakers business? I don't recall seeing anywhere that might have been a chapel of rest and so forth."

"That's because it no longer exists. After Granddad died, Dad closed the business down and sold it to a property developer who demolished the original building and built a couple of semi-detached bungalows on the plot. I can't blame him because it was in a prime position along the main road overlooking the sea."

"Anywhere near Sea View Cottage?" Hetty asked.

Simon laughed. "Yes, very near. Right next door in fact. Granddad used to live at Sea View but sold it a couple of years after he married Grandma Florence because he wanted to invest some money into her hotel. You know, up-date it and so forth and I suppose it was some of that money he gave to Dad for a deposit to buy this place."

"Well I never," exclaimed Lottie, "It seems we're following in the footsteps of your family. We stayed at Sea View Cottage for a holiday last year and that's how we came to discover Pentrillick. And now we're living in the house your parents owned. Quite spooky, I think."

Just after Simon and Sheila left to return to Tuzzy-Muzzy, Basil appeared in the hallway and asked the sisters to come and see the conversion progress before they finished work for the weekend. Hetty and Lottie happily followed Basil up the stairs and were delighted with what they saw. The stud walls were all in place and plastered and so there were now three rooms and a small hallway in the attic instead of a large void.

"And the shower room is all finished," said Lottie, running her hand across the smooth wall panels.

"Not quite," Sid held up a small cardboard box, "The taps for the wash basin aren't any good. They didn't have the ones I needed in stock so I tried these but I'm not happy with them so I'll come back and fit the right ones when they come in. Hope that's okay."

"Yes, that's fine," agreed Hetty, "because we won't use the shower room until the whole job is completely finished."

"And there isn't a door yet anyway," Lottie chuckled.

Basil pointed to three doors leaning against a wall. "We'll be doing the doors on Monday and then starting the wardrobes on Tuesday. They shouldn't take long so by the end of next week we should be finished here too."

"Lovely, and then we can paint the walls," said Lottie, "I'm really impressed by your efficiency…all three of you."

"Me too," Hetty added.

That evening, Hetty and Lottie received four more anonymous phone calls. As before, there was no-one there for the first three but on the fourth there was heavy breathing followed by a piercing scream.

"Do you think we ought to report it?" Lottie asked her sister.

Hetty shook her head. "No, I'm sure it's just kids larking around. They'll get bored eventually and do something else equally childish and pointless."

"Hmm, hopefully you're right. It might be worth asking around though to see if anyone else has been getting them."

"No, really I think it's better if we say nothing because if whoever is doing it hears people talking about the calls then they'll be inspired to continue with their silly behaviour. So much better to keep mum."

"Yes, I can see your logic and I think you're right."

Zac was up bright and early on Saturday morning, eager to meet up with his friends to prepare for the raft race which was to commence at midday. He left Primrose Cottage just before nine dressed as a pirate, and walked off down Long Lane, swishing his cardboard sword and saying 'Ahoy, there me Hearties' and 'Shiver me timbers'.

His great aunt and grandmother seated in the kitchen eating breakfast, looked wistfully after him as he left the house.

"Oh to be young again," sighed Hetty, "I'd love to take part in the raft race. It sounds fun."

"Yes, it does but I think it'll be just as enjoyable to watch and at least we'll keep dry."

"True, falling into the sea fully clothed certainly would put a damper on it in more ways than one."

Just before eleven, Hetty and Lottie, along with Grace, Simon and Sheila walked down to the village. The weather was fine although a little dull but at least the wind was light which would be beneficial to the raft race participants.

Where shall we watch?" Grace asked, as they reached the bottom of Long Lane.

"I think the pub's terrace will be as good as anywhere and we should get a good view from up there."

Simon licked his lips. "I'm game for that. I rather fancy a pint because I put too much salt on my poached eggs this morning."

"Ugh, I don't think I could face a drink this early," muttered Hetty, "I might have a coffee instead."

"You usually have a drink in the morning on Christmas Day," Lottie reminded her.

"Yes, but that's different. I'll stick to coffee."

"Me too," agreed Sheila.

"What killjoys," laughed Grace, "This is a special occasion so I shall have a glass of wine and I insist on paying for you all to have whatever you want. What would you like, Lottie?"

"I'll have a wine too, please but better make it a dry white as the red is too strong for daytime."

While Grace went to the bar to get the drinks along with Sheila to help carry them, the rest of the party went out onto the terrace where already a large crowd was gathered. Amongst them was Taffeta, dressed in jeans and T-shirt with not a bow in sight. Hetty was surprised both by outfit and her presence.

"Have you closed your tea shop for the day?" she asked.

"No, my hubby's looking after it for a couple of hours, bless him. He often does on a Saturday to give me a break. I think he rather enjoys it because he likes meeting people. Anyway, I've got to cheer on the girls."

"Which girls are they?"

"Nicki and Karen from the hairdressers," Taffeta giggled, "they're mermaids. They asked me to join them but I said I was too fat to be a mermaid."

"Too fat!" exclaimed Hetty, "there's more fat on a greasy chip."

Hetty turned her head when Grace and Sheila arrived with the drinks and she heard Grace address someone whom she clearly knew.

"Hetty, Lottie," she beckoned, "come over here and meet Malcolm and Belinda who are also staying at Tuzzy-Muzzy. Simon and Sheila have already met them because I introduced them this morning during breakfast. Malcolm is the history teacher I told you about the other day. And this is his wife, Belinda."

"Oh I see, pleased to meet you," said Hetty and Lottie. They shook hands in turn while, Grace and Sheila handed out the drinks.

"Likewise," gushed Malcolm. Belinda smiled sweetly.

"Grace told me that you recently found an old suitcase in your attic dating back to World War Two and also a little about the person to whom it must have belonged. I'd love to see it if that's alright as it sounds fascinating." Malcolm's eyes shone with enthusiasm.

"Of course, we'd be delighted to show you," said Hetty, "the more people that see it and cast an opinion the better chance we have of finding out what happened to David Tregear our mystery train driver-cum-fisherman."

Lottie laughed. "Next time Grace comes to see us you must come with her and that will probably be tomorrow as she's a frequent visitor, I'm pleased to say."

"Two boats with lots of flags on have just positioned themselves a short distance away from the shore," gushed Sheila, excitedly, "So something's happening."

Simon took several gulps of beer. "I daresay the boats will mark the spot where the rafts have to get to before they turn round and come back."

"In which case the race might be starting soon." Lottie looked at her watch, "Yes, it's nearly twelve. Let's get a bit closer, we don't want to miss anything."

Lottie moved closer to the railings to get a better view and the others all followed.

There were ten rafts in the race and every single one was bizarre. Most were built on empty oil drums; some had a wooden bottom and others it wasn't possible to see what they were based on.

"Where's your Zac?" Grace asked, casting her eyes along the beach where the rafts were lined up at the water's edge.

"He's with the pirates," gabbled Lottie, feeling proud of her grandson. "And on the raft of hippies with a tent, is our plumber Sid. He's the chap strumming a guitar."

Grace looked surprised. "Really. I wouldn't have put Sid down as being musical."

"He's not," chuckled Hetty, "He told us he can't play for toffee so we must be thankful that we're far enough away from him to hear his tuneless plonking."

"What about the Father Christmases on a sleigh?" asked Sheila, "Who are they?"

Hetty finished her coffee and placed the cup and saucer on the floor away from the many pairs of feet. "Well, I can't recognise any from here but if I remember correctly they'll be members of the Christmas Wonderland Committee. And the mermaids in the giant shell are Nicki and Karen the hairdressers with some of their friends. Taffeta was just telling me."

"Oh to be young again," said Sheila, "we didn't do things like this in my day but then I've never lived near the coast."

"Are you not from Cornwall then?" Hetty asked.

"Yes, but I've always lived in and around Truro and it's not the same as being somewhere like Pentrillick."

"Looks like they're off," Simon placed his glass of beer on the table behind him to free up his hands in order to clap and cheer.

The noise from spectators on the beach was quite deafening, especially when the first raft capsized and its vampire rowers were plunged into the water where they tried to scramble back on board. They did not succeed. Their coffin shaped raft snapped in half and the two sections drifted back towards the shore. Most other teams did not fare much better and overturned one after another.

Sid and the hippies won the raft race. Zac and his friends came third. A team of monks came second and the rest did not complete the course.

"Oh dear, I've not laughed so much for ages," chuckled Malcolm, wiping his eyes, as six soggy Santas dragged their broken sleigh onto the shore and emptied water from their Wellington boots, "I'm so glad you told us about it, Grace."

Grace nodded. "Yes, I certainly think we chose the right month to be here on holiday."

"Anyone fancy another drink?" Lottie asked, draining her empty glass as they all wandered back into the bar. "I'm paying."

"I shouldn't really but I'd like another," giggled Grace, already feeling a little light-headed, "but I actually feel in a party mood."

"Me too," Simon picked up his glass.

Sheila tutted. "But you've not finished that one yet," She pointed to the half full glass in his hand.

"I know but I had to put it down so I could clap." He quickly downed the rest of his pint. "Finished now." He put the empty glass on the bar just as Alison began to load up the glass washer. Simon glanced at the row of beer pumps. "I think I'll have a Guinness this time because that beer tasted a bit funny."

"I'm not surprised," laughed Sheila, "the amount of mints you've eaten this morning to get rid of the taste of salt."

"Malcolm, Belinda, would you like a drink?" Lottie asked.

"That's very kind," said Malcolm, "I'll have a half of Doom Bar, please."

"Tonic water for me, please," smiled Belinda.

With drinks in hand the party moved over towards a table by the fireplace where a wooden tub filled with dried hydrangeas hid the empty grate.

Simon placed his glass on the mantel piece while everyone else took a seat and to make sure there were enough chairs he borrowed a spare couple from a nearby table. Just as he was about to sit, the colour suddenly drained from his face. He groaned and put one hand over his mouth and with the other he clutched his stomach. "Oh my God. I feel sick," He doubled up in obvious pain.

Sheila leapt from her seat and grabbed his arm. "Simon," she screamed.

"Help me," he slurred. He then fell forwards and collapsed onto the floor.

Chapter Ten

On Sunday morning, Hetty and Lottie still feeling shaken by Simon's sudden illness, went to church. They left Primrose Cottage at eight thirty for the service which began at nine o'clock, leaving Zac fast asleep on the settee having been out until late the previous evening at a post raft race party.

After the service they spoke to Kitty who had played the organ and she asked if there was any news regarding the condition of Simon Berryman.

Hetty answered. "Yes, Sheila rang last night to say he was stable and that it was suspected he was suffering from food poisoning."

"Which makes us a little suspicious," blurted Lottie, "because when we were in the pub he mentioned that his beer tasted funny."

Kitty frowned. "But if the beer was off, which I doubt because Ashley is very fussy about looking after his beer correctly, then others would have been ill too because the pub must have been busy yesterday."

"You're right, it was busy," Lottie conceded, "and I suppose to be fair it could have been something he'd eaten or perhaps he picked up a bug of some sort. There always seems to be something doing the rounds."

Hetty nodded. "Yes, but whatever, at least he's alive and on the road to recovery. When he was first taken ill I thought he was a goner...he looked dreadful."

"So I've heard," sighed Kitty, "I was helping give out hot drinks to our capsized churchgoers at the time but once word got out it spread across the beach like wildfire and we'd all heard the ambulance earlier so knew something was going on."

"Oh, the church had a raft. Which one was that?" Hetty tried to recall a churchlike team other than the monks whom she knew to be members of a football team.

"The vampires," giggled Kitty.

"No, surely not." Hetty was quite taken back. "You're pulling my leg."

"I'm not. The vampires are all churchgoers and a couple are in the choir. What's more, it was Vicar Sam's idea to be vampires. He wants to get the message across that the church has a sense of humour and does not consist of narrow-minded fuddy-duddies. The youngsters love him."

"Hmm, a bit different to the last vicar then," said Hetty, looking over her shoulder to check that the new vicar was not within earshot, "he was very old-school."

Kitty nodded. "Yes, he was and I must admit I'm glad he retired."

"Well I'm surprised the new chap didn't dress up and go on the raft with them then," said Lottie. "That really would have been a sight to behold."

"Well, apparently he wanted to but unfortunately he can't swim and doesn't like being on the water." Kitty smiled. "I think he was afraid he might get seasick and he didn't want the youngsters to think him a wimp."

"But it was flat calm," Hetty stated.

"The sea was, yes," agreed Lottie, "but I should imagine it would have been pretty bumpy being on any of those rafts."

Kitty sighed. "I am so sorry I missed Simon. It was my intention to pop round and see him today. Still, never mind, these things happen. I just pray he gets well quickly and comes to visit again soon."

Zac was up and eating breakfast in the kitchen when they arrived back at Primrose Cottage.

"Did you have a good party?" Lottie asked.

"Yes, thanks, it was brill."

"Good," Lottie reached for the kettle.

"How's Simon?" Zac asked, "I heard he was taken ill."

"Yes, he was and it looks like it was food poisoning," said Hetty, as she slipped off her sandals, "but he's on the mend."

Zac frowned. "So what did he eat? I mean, as far as I know no-one else got food poisoning yesterday. Not bad enough to be taken to hospital anyway."

"Yes, Kitty said something along those lines."

"I think it all sounds very dodgy," Zac's face was set in a frown, "Have the police been notified?"

"Why? You're not suggesting he might have been deliberately poisoned, are you, Zac?"

"I'm not really suggesting anything. I just think it's a bit odd. That's all."

Hetty looked concerned. "Well if it was deliberate then whoever did it must have had a reason and since Simon is not a local, not now anyway, the only possible reason I can think of is that it must be something to do with David Tregear's disappearance."

Lottie switched on the kettle. "Meaning someone might be trying to prevent any further investigations or something like that. Surely not."

"But why would they?" Zac asked. "I mean, if that were the case then whoever the poisoner was would be after you two rather than Simon. After all you're the ones with the suitcase and the ones asking all the questions."

"Yes, but Simon is a Berryman and so has some knowledge of the family history, whereas we just know what we've been told." Hetty put on her slippers, "Perhaps someone's trying to shut him up in case he suddenly remembers something relevant."

"But that would suggest something sinister happened to David," gasped Lottie.

Hetty sat down at the kitchen table. "Perhaps it did and that's why there's no trace of him."

"You mean someone might have murdered David," chortled Zac, "I think that's highly unlikely although I suppose these things happen."

Hetty's face was white. "It would certainly explain the hidden suitcase."

Lottie poured water into three mugs for coffee. "And if we're on the right trail it would figure that whoever was guilty started the story that David had run away to avoid conscription in order to cover their tracks."

"I don't like it," grumbled Hetty.

Lottie agreed. "Me neither and I've just thought of something else. The weird phone calls. They could have come from the same person who attempted to poison Simon."

"If he was deliberately poisoned." When Hetty sipped her coffee she was conscious that her heart was beating much faster than normal. "Let's hope it was something he ate which didn't agree with him. Maybe he has an allergy that he was unaware of."

Lottie laughed. "But I thought you liked solving murder mysteries, Het."

"I do but not when they're this close to home."

When Grace called round later that morning they told her of the theory they had discussed with Zac. The colour drained from her face. "That's a horrible thought. I do hope you're wrong."

"I expect we are," said Hetty, who was beginning to warm to the idea, "but it's fun to speculate and it makes our probing much more exciting."

"I agree," laughed Lottie, "and for that reason I think we ought to get a white board so that we can write down all the facts and do some serious investigating."

Hetty nodded. "Good idea. And the first thing we need to find out is if anyone back in 1942 had a motive to um…dispose of David."

Grace looked shocked. "But do you think we ought? After all if someone has already tried to kill Simon because they thought he knew something then they might give us the same treatment."

"Hmm, that's quite a good reason," said Hetty, drumming her fingers on the arm of her chair, "actually it's a very good reason but I think it's hardly likely we'll discover anything useful because there's nothing really we can look into for clues, is there? So as far as I'm concerned it's just a bit of harmless fun. Besides no-one will know, will they?"

Grace had to smile. "But half the village already knows that you're trying to find out what happened to David Tregear."

"That's true," Lottie agreed, "and I don't think there are many secrets in this village that Tess doesn't know about."

"Who's Tess?" Grace asked.

Lottie chuckled. "She's a very nice lady who likes to keep up with the latest news."

"And then share it," Hetty added.

"You've probably seen her because she's currently working part-time in Taffeta's Tea Shoppe and no doubt somewhere else as well. It's often tricky to keep track of her." Lottie noticed that the old bear had fallen onto the floor.

"Sounds like she's someone to interrogate then," laughed Grace. "She might even know something."

Lottie picked up the bear and sat him on her lap. "Be nice to think she did but I doubt it unless she's a descendant of the Tregears or Berrymans and from what we've discovered so far I think that's highly unlikely."

"I've just realised Malcolm and Belinda aren't with you," commented Hetty.

"No, I told them I was coming round but they said since it was such a beautiful morning they thought they'd go and tour the Lizard Peninsula." Grace laughed, "I think they'll save visiting you for a rainy day."

"Can't blame them for that," said Hetty.

"We've never been to the Lizard Peninsula, have we, Het? I think we ought to put it on our bucket list."

Grace laughed. "Do you have one?"

"No, but it's what people say these days, isn't it? To be honest I am quite happy to just plod along and take each day as it comes but then I never have been very adventurous."

"Anyway, back to the investigation," insisted Hetty, slightly annoyed that she had caused them to deviate from their project, "I think rather than wait until we have a white board we must start writing down facts on a good old sheet of paper." She turned to her sister, "Do we have any large sheets, Lottie?"

"Lining paper," suggested Lottie, as she stood up, sat the bear on the table and headed towards the door, "there's a good half roll of it in the cupboard under the stairs. I'll go and get it."

With a large section of lining paper pinned to the wall, the three ladies tried to think what to write.

"Put a line down the middle and then head each side with the names of the two families," said Lottie to Hetty who held the felt tipped pen.

Hetty wrote Tregear on one side of the paper and Berryman on the other. "Now what?" she asked.

"Write down on the relevant sides all family members who were still living in 1942 because that seems to be the year when David went missing. I refer to the fact he wasn't at his brother's funeral," said Lottie.

While Hetty wrote down names Grace tapped her fingers on the side of her coffee mug. "What about a girlfriend? I mean, he was thirty years old and a nice looking lad so he must have had a girlfriend. In which case she might in some way give us a motive. What do you think?"

"Hmm," mused Lottie, "it's not a bad idea but there's no way we could find that out so it's not really possible to chase it up."

"I don't know, I think we ought to pursue it," Hetty agreed. "I mean, it could be that David stole another chap's girl and the cheated chappie took exception."

"And did what?" Lottie asked.

"Murdered him of course," whispered Hetty, "after all that's the reason for our current investigation and the white board."

"Lining paper," corrected Lottie, "white board sounds too official and if I'm honest, murder seems a bit extreme as well, especially if we're trying to pin it on some bloke who'd lost his girlfriend to another man."

Hetty tutted. "Stop putting spanners in the works, Lottie Burton. At this stage we're only toying with ideas."

"Humph, a few hours ago you chose to believe Simon's poisoning was something he ate and that no-one was trying to silence him now you're seriously treating David's disappearance as a murder investigation."

"We're on safe ground," snapped Hetty, "because we're talking of something that happened seventy five years ago so the murderer would almost certainly be dead. What's more I think you're getting cold feet, Lottie and becoming a cowardy-custard."

Grace giggled and then on seeing Hetty's stern look turned it into a cough.

"Anyway, never mind the whys and wherefores. How can we find out if David had a girlfriend?" Hetty asked.

"We can't," hissed Lottie, emphatically, "I've already said that because she, like the murderer, if there was one, will be dead."

Grace tried to look serious. "Okay, so let's assume David was murdered by a rival. For now that gives us a motive but another question we need to answer is what would said murderer have done with the body?"

Lottie's face looked blank.

Hetty looked thoughtful and then suddenly gasped. "I know. Perhaps the murderer broke into the Berryman's chapel of rest the night before Peter's funeral and put David in the coffin along with his brother. That way he'd never be found and it would explain why David wasn't at his brother's funeral."

Grace chuckled "But he would have been there if he were in the coffin."

Hetty scowled. "It's no laughing matter, Grace Dunkerley."

"You mean, you're serious?"

"Absolutely."

"Whoops, sorry."

"I agree with Grace, it's a ridiculous idea," spluttered Lottie, "for a start there wouldn't be enough room. You read too many mystery books, Het."

Hetty obstinately shook her head. "I disagree. I'm sure Harold Berryman would have insisted his stepson's coffin was of the very best quality and bigger and sturdier than most. Remember it was wartime too and because of food rationing people had less to eat then so the brothers were probably both quite skinny."

"Yes, it was wartime," said Lottie, "and I think you'll find that wood was rationed like lots of other things and instead of

Harold being able to give his stepson a supersonic coffin it would have been simple, thin and lightweight."

Hetty scowled. "Up-country no doubt but this is Cornwall remember. Anyway, I daresay Harold could have got hold of some wood on the black market and made a nice coffin and from the outside no-one would have been able to tell whether it was thin or not."

"It'd weigh more if it was made with a thicker wood," Lottie persisted.

Grace laughed. "Especially if there were two people in it as you suggest."

Hetty scowled unable to come up with a satisfactory reply.

"Anyway," gushed Lottie, "going back to what you said a few minutes ago, Het. If someone had broken into the funeral parlour and popped David in with Peter, the police would have been called to investigate the break-in."

Grace nodded. "Yes, they would."

"Hmm, must have been an inside job then," reasoned Hetty, tapping her foot as she thought.

"An inside job," spluttered Lottie, "that's not possible because only Simon's father, George and his Auntie Polly worked at the funeral parlour and David wouldn't have stolen the girlfriends of either."

"Do you think Polly might have had a girlfriend then?" Grace asked.

Lottie shrugged her shoulders. "Who knows what they got up to back then?"

"Harold Berryman worked there too when it was busy," Hetty reminded them.

"And he was happily married to his second wife, Florence," reasoned Lottie.

"There must have been someone else then," persisted Hetty.

Lottie shook her head. "But as far as we know it was just run by the family."

"There was someone else," gasped Hetty, as she leaned forward in her chair, "we've forgotten about the farm worker chappie who drove the hearse. Remember, Simon mentioned him and not only did he work on a farm and drive the hearse he was also crew on the lifeboat with David *and* he lodged here in this house with George, meaning he would have had access to the attic."

Lottie's eyes were like saucers. "You could be right and I bet the hearse driver was old Jimmy."

Chapter Eleven

On Monday morning, Hetty, Lottie and Zac moved things back into Zac's room after Basil and Mark had carried up the heavier items of furniture. The freshly plastered ceiling was completely dry and looked as smooth as silk but it was decided not to paint it until September when Zac had gone home because they felt he had slept on the settee for long enough. There was also no carpet on the floor but Lottie took the rug from the dining room to put beside his bed.

Just as Hetty reached the bottom of the stairs to check that they had not forgotten anything, the doorbell rang. It was a delivery man with the pond liner. At Hetty's request, he dropped it in the hallway at the foot of the stairs.

"Thank you, that's very kind of you," said Hetty as she eagerly signed for the consignment.

"No problem." As the delivery man retreated down the doorstep he turned, looked back and chuckled. "Lovely clump of pampas grass you've got there." And to Hetty's horror, he winked.

"That horrible grass has to go," muttered Hetty to herself as she quickly closed the door. When she caught sight of her reflection in the hall mirror, she was shocked to see that her cheeks were a bright crimson.

Once everything was back in Zac's room and his bed was made, Hetty and Lottie carried the liner out into the back garden and laid it down beside the carpeted pond. Zac was already out there cutting the grass. Hetty thought about repeating the incident with the delivery man but changed her mind knowing her sister and Zac would most likely laugh.

"I think we'll wait for Grace to visit before we attempt to put it in," remarked Hetty, "after all three brains are better than two. Besides, I know she'll want to help because she's as excited about our pond as we are."

"True and she's bound to come round this afternoon to see if there's any more news."

"I agree, so let's have some lunch now and then if she's not here by two, I'll send her a text and ask her to come and give us a hand."

"Well, if there are going to be three of you to put the liner in you won't need me," reasoned Zac, as he wound up the lawn mower's cable, "so will it be alright if I take Albert out? Emma's coming round in a minute so we'll take him for a nice long walk."

Hetty looked down at Albert whose tail was wagging nineteen to the dozen having heard the word walk. "I would very much appreciate it. The little fellow could do with some exercise but by the time we've finished here today I'll be too knackered to take him any further than the end of the lane and back."

"Brilliant. I'll just grab a sandwich then and when Em gets here we'll be off."

By late afternoon the liner was in place and water was pouring into the black shiny pond through the hosepipe.

"Do you have any large stones lying around?" Grace asked. "Because once the pond is full we'll need to lay them round the outside to cover the edges and make it look tidy."

"We'd already thought of that," said Lottie, proudly, "You'll find a fairly big pile of stones in all shapes and sizes at the top of the garden near the compost heap. They're from the wall at the end of the garden which has part fallen down but we won't need them all because we've decided to have the wall much lower when it's rebuilt so that we can see into the field when we're in the garden."

"Brilliant, let's go and fetch them down."

When the pond was full and the stones were artistically laid, the ladies sat with mugs of tea admiring their handiwork.

"Strange but it's fascinating to watch even with nothing in it other than reflections," whispered Hetty, "It's really calming."

"There's something in it now," chuckled Lottie, "Look, there's a water boatman swimming on the surface."

"Talking of boatmen, is there any news yet about David's boat?" Grace asked.

"Sadly not," said Lottie, "Every time the phone rings I hope it'll be Bernie with good news but so far there's been nothing. Still it's early days yet and the boat might not even be in Cornwall now."

"Or if it is it might be in a garden somewhere full of flowers," suggested Hetty.

Lottie laughed. "No, Het. The Goliath was a fishing boat so it'd be far too big to fill with plants. Boats used to display flowers are usually little rowing boats or punts."

"My goodness me, look at the time," Grace sprang to her feet, "I must go back and change. I'm going out for a meal with the Jacksons tonight."

"Very nice," said Lottie.

Grace tilted her head to one side as she stood to leave. "Is that the phone I can hear?"

"Yes, it is," Hetty ran indoors to catch it before it stopped ringing. When she picked up the receiver she was delighted to hear the voice of Bernie the Boatman. "Talk of the devil. We were just chatting about you and the Goliath."

Bernie chuckled. "Well, I never because that's why I'm ringing. I've found it, you see. Of all places it's in one of the

Liddicott-Treen's out-buildings at Pentrillick House and has been there since the nineteen seventies."

"Really. I wonder what it's doing up there."

"Well apparently Tristan's father bought it at an auction of fishing boats and equipment with every intention of doing it up, but he never got round to it and it has remained untouched ever since."

"That's wonderful news. Do you think we could go and see it?"

"Yes, Tristan said to give him a ring when you want to go up there and he'll show it to you himself."

"I shall ring straight away. Thank you so much, Bernie. We really appreciate it. You're a star."

"My pleasure."

"Has Grace gone?" Hetty asked, as she returned to the garden.

"Yes, she said to say goodbye."

"Oh, never mind we can tell her the news when we next see her." She then told Lottie the nature of the phone call. After discussing it briefly the sisters decided to view the boat the following day and Hetty rang Tristan to see if that was possible; it was. She then phoned the hairdressers and made an appointment to have her hair cut. Something she had been meaning to do for several days.

After a brief discussion, Zac and Emma decided to take Albert along the main street of Pentrillick and out into the open countryside, then down the lane which led to Pentrillick House.

"I see the blackberries are ripening," said Emma, as they passed brambles laden with fruit in the hedgerow, "I must tell Mum because she loves making blackberry and apple jam."

"And I expect you like eating it," Zac teased.

"Hmm…yes, but strawberry is my favourite especially if it's homemade."

"I like apricot but then I'm pretty fond of raspberry too."

Emma laughed. "What would the others say if they could hear us talking about jam?"

"They'd say we were nuts. Still, they're not here so it doesn't matter."

"No, anyway, is there any more news yet about that poor chap who was taken ill on Raft Race day? What poisoned him, I mean."

Zac shook his head. "No, and there's no indication as to what the poison was but I do know he's a lot better. We think it's a bit odd, I mean it could have been something he ate or drank but then again there's always the possibility that someone might have slipped something in his drink at the pub. Don't laugh but Grandma and Auntie Het are treating David Tregear's disappearance as a murder investigation."

Emma laughed. "Sorry, but why?"

"Because if Simon was deliberately poisoned they reckon whoever did it was trying to shut him up. Simon being a Berryman."

Emma tutted. "That's crazy. Whatever put that idea into their heads?"

"Not what but who. It was me you see. I sort of said it jokingly but they've taken it seriously. At least Auntie Het has. I'm not so sure about Grandma as I think she's more level headed."

"Okay, so just for a laugh who might have poisoned Simon?"

"Now that's the sixty four million dollar question."

"Isn't it just, and did you say they suspect it was done in the pub?"

"Yes, they believe his drink was tampered with during the race."

Emma frowned. "In which case your gran and aunt must have some idea of who it might have been as they were with him at that time."

"I don't think they've really given that much thought. They seem more interested in finding out who killed David Tregear even though there's not a shred of evidence to suggest that he was murdered."

"Except for the fact his suitcase was hidden."

"Spot on."

"I wonder if we can help in any way."

"Hmm, it's a pity we weren't in the pub when Simon keeled over because if we had been we'd be able to toss around a few names of people in the vicinity."

"Well, we can do it the other way round, I suppose," laughed Emma, "What I mean is, we know who wasn't in the pub because they were on the beach."

"Which in retrospect seemed to be just about the whole village."

"Exactly, so who might it have been? Do you know who your gran and aunt were with, other than the chap who was poisoned, that is?"

"Simon, he's the chap who was poisoned and with him was his wife Sheila. Then there was Grace, you know, she's staying in the guest house next door. I think Tommy and Kitty were with them too. No, no, forget that because Kitty was on the beach cheering on the vampires."

"Who didn't even get half way round the course."

"And they weren't the only ones."

"So were Sheila, Simon and Grace the only ones with your gran and aunt?"

"Yes, no, no I'd forgotten the Jacksons. They didn't go down with them but met them while they were there."

"Who are the Jacksons?"

"A couple who are staying at the guest house next door. I don't know their Christian names and I've not met them but Grace was telling Grandma and Auntie Het that they'd like to see the suitcase because they're interested in history or something like that."

Emma sighed. "I see, so really they were all friends. Well, acquaintances anyway."

"Yes, but anyone could have slipped something in Simon's drink when the race was on because apparently he'd put his glass down on the table behind him."

Emma groaned. "So unless Ashley and Alison have CCTV cameras in the pub there's no way of telling who it might have been."

"Precisely and as it happens I know the police have asked Ashley about CCTV because Kyle told me."

"And do they have it?"

Zac shook his head. "Regrettably not."

"Oh dear, it doesn't look like we can be of any help after all then."

The following morning as Hetty and Lottie were getting ready to go to Pentrillick House, Grace called to see them.

"Oh, are you off out somewhere?" she asked, observing the sisters were both in the hallway and wearing shoes instead their usual slippers.

Hetty opened the door wide. "Yes, but do come in because we're not quite ready."

Lottie nodded in agreement. "We have to make coffee for Basil and Mark before we go otherwise we'll be in trouble. Normally Zac makes it if we go out but he's out himself. He's gone kayaking with Emma and Kyle."

"So are you going anywhere nice or just shopping?" Grace was curious.

"We're going to Pentrillick House because Bernie has tracked down David's boat, you know, Goliath and so we're eager to see it. Not that seeing it will shed any light on the mystery."

"I'll go and make the coffee while you chat to Grace," Lottie went into the kitchen.

"Okay." Hetty turned back to face Grace. "As I just said the boat's at Pentrillick House and apparently has been for a good many years. We're meeting Tristan Liddicott-Treen there at twelve. Apparently the boat was bought at an auction by his late father who intended to restore it but never got round to it."

"It's probably in quite a bad way then after all this time," said Grace, "if it's been neglected, that is."

"Yes, I expect it is, even though it will have been under cover all the time it's been at Pentrillick House."

"Anyway, if you're off out I'll leave you to get on." Grace turned towards the door.

"No, no, don't go. Come with us? You can have a look around the house and grounds then as it's well worth seeing. We can have lunch in the café too."

"Are you sure?" Grace seemed hesitant, "I mean, I'd love to go with you but don't want you to feel obliged to ask me just because I'm here."

"Don't be silly, of course we don't mind. It'd be nice to have your company and I'm sure you're probably as keen to help solve this mystery as we are."

"True, but just give me a minute to pop back to get my jacket and handbag. If we're having lunch out I insist on paying."

Hetty suggested that Lottie should drive and that Grace should sit in the front passenger seat. As the car left the drive and turned into Blackberry Way, Grace asked if the police had had any luck finding out how Simon had been poisoned.

"No luck whatsoever," said Hetty, as Tommy with Kitty emerged round the corner with Fagan on his lead. All three ladies waved to the walkers. "Nor do I expect there to be," Hetty continued, "I mean, there's nothing really to go on with all traces of his beer lost because his glass had been washed and as far as what he ate that day, Sheila reckons they both ate pretty much the same."

"Well yes, and they had breakfast at Tuzzy-Muzzy and the other guests, myself included, are all fine," reflected Grace.

"And I don't think the police are taking it that seriously anyway because the poison wasn't anywhere near enough to kill him," added Lottie.

Hetty leaned back and fastened her seat belt. "As for trying to find out if David had a girlfriend or who drove the hearse for the Berrymans and lodged at Primrose Cottage with George, we've got absolutely nowhere because there's simply no-one to ask. It's most frustrating. If only we had some names to go on although there's always the possibility that the hearse driver was old Jimmy to whom Peter referred on the postcard but as for a girlfriend that's a no goer."

"Perhaps Simon will suddenly remember the hearse driver's name," said Grace, trying to be positive. "You know it'll suddenly come to him in the middle of the night, like things do."

"We can but hope," laughed Hetty.

The car wound its way down the hill and as it neared the bottom of Long Lane Lottie applied the brakes but to her horror they appeared to be ineffectual. She tried again but the car continued to gather speed.

"The brakes are not working," she screamed, slamming her foot repeatedly on the pedal, "oh my God, the brakes are not working."

"Use the hand brake," Hetty shouted, as she tried with trembling fingers to unfasten her seatbelt. But Lottie's screams drowned out her words and Grace seemed to have gone into a trance.

As the car hurtled towards the bottom of the hill, Lottie half closed her eyes and, clutching the steering wheel, prepared to turn quickly right to avoid crashing into the Crown and Anchor opposite. Meanwhile, coming along the street at a steady pace was a lorry. As the car shot out of the lane in front of it, the lorry driver slammed on his brakes. He skidded and missed the car with just inches to spare. Lottie was a trembling wreck as the car drew level with the pub's car park and abruptly stopped. Hetty, having finally released her seatbelt, had stretched her arm in between the front seats and pulled on the hand brake.

The driver of the lorry, himself badly shaken, jumped from his cab and hurled abuse at Lottie who covered her face and burst into tears. Meanwhile, Hetty seated in the back wound down the window and told him what had happened.

Alison Rowe, Landlady of the Crown and Anchor, was out in the pub's smoking area sweeping the floor when she heard the lorry screech to a halt and the screams and shouting that followed. Realising someone was in trouble, she tossed the broom to one side and ran to see if anyone was hurt. She found all three passengers trembling with fear and wiping tears from their eyes. The lorry driver feeling his legs might give way was sitting on the kerb. Before Alison attempted to help the ladies out of the vehicle she called into the pub for others to help escort the shaken passengers inside the building. She then asked the lorry driver if he was alright.

"Yes, thanks, love. I'm okay now. The old ticker's beginning to slow back down and there's no damage done."

"Can I get you a coffee or something?"

"No, no I'm fine, honestly and I really ought to be getting on my way." He stood up. "I hope the ladies are alright and please tell the driver I'm sorry I shouted. I didn't realise her brakes weren't working."

"Of course," Alison watched the lorry drive away and then went into the pub to relay the message. She found the ladies sitting in the warm sunshine on the terrace with glasses of brandy given to them by Ashley. After hearing from the ladies what had happened, Alison phoned Vince Royale who owned the garage on the outskirts of the village so that he could pick up the car with his breakdown truck and establish what was wrong with the brakes. She also suggested the ladies seek medical help for all seemed badly shaken but they declined and insisted they were already feeling much better. However, Hetty did make a phone call to Pentrillick House to let Tristan Liddicott-Treen know what had happened and to apologise for having to cancel the viewing of the boat.

Vince Royale came out with his rescue vehicle and took the car back to his garage. He told the sisters they could have a courtesy car while he looked into the problem. Hetty thanked him and said not to worry as they could always take the bus and it was good to walk anyway. However, Alison thought it unwise for the ladies to walk home as all three seemed a little unsteady and so she drove them back to Blackberry Way herself.

Later in the afternoon, as Hetty and Lottie sat on the doorstep in the front garden of Primrose Cottage, a police car pulled up by their gates. Grace was not with them; she had returned to Tuzzy-Muzzy to lie down. Two police officers stepped from the car. Both sisters stood up concerned that something might be wrong.

"Good afternoon, ladies. We're here about the near accident you had this morning." voiced the older of the two policemen. "How are you feeling?"

"Fine, fine," gushed Lottie, "aren't we, Het?

Hetty nodded. "Yes, we are now. Would you like a cup of tea? We were just thinking of having one."

"That would be very nice, thank you."

All four went indoors.

"Please excuse the banging," urged Lottie, seeing both police officers look upwards, "we're having a loft conversion done."

"Very nice too," said the younger officer, "you have lovely views up here."

When the tea was made and they were all seated in the sitting room, Hetty and Lottie were told that the brakes on their car had been tampered with.

Hetty's face turned white. "Are you sure? I mean, we'd assumed the car's brakes failed through wear and tear or whatever but if it's true that they were tampered with then it looks as though someone was trying to kill us."

"Or frighten us," Lottie added, unwilling to accept her sister's surmise.

"Precisely," agreed the older officer, "and for those reasons I need to know if there is anyone who might wish to harm either or both of you?"

"Well no," declared Hetty, "we've only been living here since early December and as far as we know we've not made any enemies. But I must admit it's a little unnerving that this should have happened to us so soon after what happened to Simon Berryman the other day."

"And then there's the phone calls too," blurted Lottie, "I wouldn't be at all surprised if they're not linked as well."

"Phone calls?" queried the younger officer, "perhaps you'd like to tell us more."

Lottie explained about the phone calls. The younger officer took down notes and said that they would arrange for calls on their phone line to be intercepted in order to trace their source.

"Are you friends with Mr Berryman?" asked the older officer, "because I believe you were with him when he was taken ill?"

Hetty nodded. "That's right, we were but we've only known him for a week or so. He used to live here you see, many years ago and we got in touch with him hoping he might know something about the suitcase we found in the attic and what happened to its owner, David Tregear who appears to have disappeared without trace back in the nineteen forties."

"A suitcase and a missing person," repeated the older officer, "perhaps you'd like to elaborate on that."

Hetty stood up. "Okay. You start the story, Lottie, while I fetch the suitcase."

Following the meeting with Hetty and Lottie, the police spent some time accumulating evidence regarding the possible poisoning of Mr Simon Berryman, the tampering of the brakes on Ms Henrietta Tonkin's car and the anonymous phone calls to Ms Tonkins and her sister Mrs Burton.

They also looked into the possibility that David Tregear, a train driver, was murdered by an unknown man who drove the hearse for the Berryman family's funeral business of whom they could find no records but who might possibly have been called Jimmy.

Further investigations established there was also no record of David Tregear having been reported missing; not that this was unusual for many people disappeared during wartime to avoid conscription. However, in the case of David Tregear there was never any risk of him being called up because of his occupation on the railway. Furthermore, David appeared to have vanished within days of his twin brother's death and had not attended the funeral: a suspicious occurrence as the brothers were said to be very close. There was also the fact that a suitcase containing the belongings of the missing man were found hidden beneath the floorboards in the attic of a house in which the hearse driver - possibly called Jimmy - had allegedly lived during the time of David Tregear's disappearance. Also residing in the house was its owner a Mr George Berryman who ran the family funeral business in Pentrillick at which the hearse driver - possibly called Jimmy - was employed. Furthermore, George Berryman was also the father of the poisoned man, Simon Berryman.

After all the evidence was gathered, the police decided there was sufficient justification to apply for an Exhumation Licence regarding the remains of Peter Tregear to ascertain if the remains of his missing brother, David Tregear, were also in the coffin as suggested by Ms Tonkins and Mrs Burton following his murder by the unnamed hearse driver who had access to the funeral parlour and the coffin due to the nature of his part-time employment.

Chapter Twelve

On Wednesday morning, in order to take their minds off the probability of Peter Tregear's remains being exhumed, Hetty and Lottie, still without their car, took the bus to Rosudgeon to have a look around the car boot sale which took place at the Sports and Social Club weekly from March until October. They didn't want anything in particular but always enjoyed a rummage through the stalls as you never knew what might turn up. It was as they were looking at plants that Lottie spotted a fuchsia named Taffeta Bow.

"Look at this," she chuckled, holding up the plant so that Hetty might see the label, "I must get it and give it to Taffeta."

"That's a lovely idea," Hetty agreed, "well spotted. In fact get two because I should like one as well."

After they had browsed most of the stalls they made their way back across the busy field towards the bus stop; but as they passed a stall decked out with colourful balls of wool and a neat pile of knitting patterns, Lottie stopped, eager to see if there were any of interest. While her sister looked through the patterns, Hetty walked further along the aisle to a car where pictures were laid out in stacks on the ground and protected from the damp by a huge sheet of plastic. Wondering if there might be anything suitable to hang in the new bedrooms when they were finished, Hetty knelt down to take a look. Several were too large, others were modern and didn't appeal nor did ones depicting cars and motor bikes. Flowers she liked and also the landscapes. Portraits were of no interest because the subjects were strangers. But then a name caught her eye. A name on the bottom of an oil painting of a man, just head and shoulders wearing a chunky navy blue jumper and a black flat cap. His hair was grey as were his moustache and beard. In the corner of his mouth was a pipe. The name on the picture was Old Jimmy.

Hetty stood and held up the picture; her hands were trembling. "How much?" she asked, trying to suppress the excitement in her voice.

"To you, five quid, darling."

Hetty didn't quibble and pulled a five pound note from her purse.

"Thanks," said the stall holder, "have a nice day."

"And you," Hetty nodded politely and ran off to find her sister.

"Hmm, interesting," Lottie agreed, as the stall holder selling the wool handed her fifty pence change, "but it's hardly likely to be the old Jimmy who drove the hearse."

Hetty scowled. "What makes you so sure?"

"Well Jimmy's hardly an unusual name. What's more you don't even know that it was painted in Cornwall."

"The sea is in the background," reasoned Hetty.

Lottie laughed. "Sorry, Het, but we live on an island and so are surrounded by the sea."

"I still think it's our old Jimmy because he looks a bit like a fisherman and I should imagine the lifeboat chappies and the fishermen dressed in a similar way."

"And you may well be right but I doubt it." Lottie dropped two knitting patterns and a large quantity of wool into her shopping bag. "Anyway, I'm finished here so if you are too we can go home."

Hetty nodded. "Yes, and there's a bus due in ten minutes so we can catch that."

The bus stop in Pentrillick was quite near to Taffeta's Tea Shoppe and so they went straight in there after leaving the bus as both were gasping for a cup of tea and they wanted to give Taffeta the fuchsia. As they sat down, Lottie hid the plants under the table because she didn't want to give Taffeta her gift until after they'd had their tea in case the proprietor thought they were after free beverages. Hence when they stood to leave, Taffeta was overwhelmed with her surprise present.

"Well, I never. Fancy there being a fuchsia called Taffeta Bow. Thank you so much. You're so kind. I shall give it pride of place on the window sill."

Like an excited child she took a saucer from the stack on the counter and placed plant on saucer half way between the curtains.

Hetty decided rather than have Lottie pour more scorn on her purchase, to put the painting of Old Jimmy in her bedroom out of sight while she thought of a way to try and establish who he was. Not that Lottie would have noticed the painting had she hung it on the sitting room wall for she was completely engrossed in her knitting patterns and was sorting through her vast collection of needles in order to start knitting a complicated looking cardigan in daffodil yellow.

Half an hour after they had arrived home, the doorbell rang. Hetty answered it and was surprised to see the new vicar standing on the doorstep.

"Oh, hello, Vicar."

"Good afternoon, Miss Tonkins. I bumped into Tess this morning and she told me about your accident. I've called to see how you and your sister are."

"How kind," smiled Hetty, stepping aside, "would you like to come in for a cup of tea?"

"Yes, thank you. That would be very nice."

Lottie put her knitting aside as the vicar entered the sitting room. "Vicar, how lovely to see you." She stood up and shook his hand.

They drank tea from seldom used bone china teacups, part of a set which Lottie had received as a wedding present back in the nineteen seventies. And as the sisters made small talk with the vicar with whom they felt ill at ease because they hardly knew him, Zac peeped his head around the door.

"Hi, Zac," gushed the vicar. His face brightened up.

"Hi, Sam. What are you doing here?"

"I've come to see your um…um…."

"Grandma and great aunt," finished Zac.

"Yes, that's right. I've just heard about the accident, you see."

"Hmm, not good," tutted Zac, "anyway, great to see you, Sam. I'm off down to the beach now for a swim."

The vicar laughed. "I won't tell a lie and say I envy you."

Hetty tutted. "I should hope not, Vicar."

The vicar frowned.

"My reference was to you telling a lie," stated Hetty, keen to clarify her reprimand.

"Oh yes, yes of course. I see."

"I remember last summer when we were all on holiday," said Lottie to Zac, "that you weren't at all keen on swimming either."

"No, I wasn't but I rather like it now. Anyway, must go. Catch you all later."

"Smashing lad," said the vicar, as the front door closed. He finished his tea and placed the cup down on its saucer. "And I must be going too. I've a young couple coming to see me this afternoon about getting married." He stood up.

"A wedding, how lovely." Hetty rose to her feet. "I'll see you out."

While Hetty escorted the vicar towards the door, Lottie placed the teacups and saucers on a tray and carried it into the kitchen.

"Thank you for calling," smiled Hetty, as the vicar stepped outside. "It was very kind of you." She gave a regal wave.

"The pleasure was all mine, Miss Tonkins, and I'm glad to have found you both well."

Hetty felt her face flush when he glanced towards the pampas grass and held her breath in case he made a comment but to her relief he merely nodded his head and said: "Perhaps we'll see you in church on Sunday."

"Yes," gushed Hetty, "we shall do our best to be there."

"Splendid. Good day."

"Good day."

"Why does the vicar talk formally to us but sort of all trendy like when he's talking to youngsters," grumbled Hetty, as she went into the kitchen where Lottie was preparing lunch, "it makes me feel like an old fuddy-duddy."

Lottie laughed. "It must be very difficult for him, Het, being new I mean and not knowing people very well. I suppose he's afraid ladies of our years might take offence if addressed by our Christian names and it doesn't help that when in his presence we both speak in our best telephone voices."

Hetty was taken back. "I wasn't speaking in a telephone voice, was I?"

"Yes, you were and so was I," Lottie laughed, "and I nearly died when I saw you'd used my old tea set."

Hetty bit her bottom lip. "It seemed the right thing to do but then I'm not used to being called on by vicars."

"Me neither but if it happens again I say we must try and be ourselves."

"You're right, and next time we go to church and get a chance to speak to him we must insist he calls us by our

Christian names. That way he'll know that we're not old stick-in-the-muds."

"And that we drink tea from mugs like everybody else."

In the afternoon Sheila Berryman phoned to say that Simon was much improved and that he would be coming out of hospital the next day.

"Oh, that's a relief," sighed Lottie, who had answered the phone. "We'll pop over and see you when we get the car back."

"Well actually, I was going to suggest we come to see you. It'll do Simon good to get out and about and I know he's eager to show you the old photos even though they're not very good."

"Even better," agreed Lottie, "and you can see our pond. Not that there's anything much in it yet other than water."

"I shall look forward to that."

"Let us know when you'd like to visit and I'll make sure we're in. Het's not here at the moment, she's gone to have her hair cut."

When Hetty took a seat in the hairdressers she noticed that Natalie Burleigh who with her husband, Luke, rented Fuchsia Cottage in Blackberry Way, was in the next chair also having her hair cut. Hetty smiled at the younger woman who smiled back in return.

"How's your research going?" asked hairdresser Karen, as she pinned up Hetty's hair.

"How come you know about that?" Hetty was clearly surprised.

Karen smiled. "There's not much goes on this village that's not discussed in here. Isn't that so, Nicki?" she said to the woman doing Natalie's hair.

"Absolutely. I reckon I could write a book based on the gossip I've heard in here."

Hetty chuckled. "Best be careful what I say then."

"Seriously though," said Karen, "have you been able to track down any Tregears? I think that's the name we were told you're looking for."

"Yes, you're right it is and no we've not been able to find any but then we think that's because there are none to find. You see, it looks very much as though the Tregears who ran the Pentrillick Hotel left no descendants. More's the shame."

"Oh dear, so you've come to a dead end?"

"Not entirely, because Florence Tregear, the mother of David, the missing train driver-cum-fisherman, married again to a chap called Harold Berryman. So we're looking at Berrymans now."

"That's interesting," remarked Natalie, "because my husband's mother's maiden name was Berryman."

Hetty's eyes opened wide. "Really! Does he come from round here then because we have reason to believe it's a local name?"

"Is it? Well fancy that. But no, Luke was born and bred in Rochdale." She smiled sweetly, "So was I for that matter."

"But his ancestors might have lived in Cornwall," Hetty persisted, "I mean, what made you want to live down here? Perhaps Luke was drawn back to his roots."

"The sea," laughed Natalie, "that's what drew us down here. Luke's keen to learn to surf so when he saw a job advertised down here he applied for it and to his delight got it." She saw the inquisitive looks on Hetty's face in the mirror and answered the next question before it was asked. "He's a teacher," she revealed, "science is his subject and very good at it he is too."

"Ugh," groaned Karen, "I hated everything about science when I was at school."

"Me too," Nicki agreed.

"Ah," tutted Hetty, as the penny dropped, "that's why he's not working at present, because it's the school's summer holiday."

Natalie nodded. "Correct, and we're currently looking for a house to buy because Fuchsia Cottage is just a stopgap. We were thinking of going to Penzance but rather like Pentrillick so hope something might crop up here this summer. I especially would like to live here because apart from it being lovely I'm told the village holds excellent aerobics classes."

"That's right," enthused Hetty, "they've stopped for the summer though and start up again in September."

"That's what I was told by Mrs Mannering."

"Yes, young Emma's mum. She runs it."

"I've heard on the grapevine that Sea View Cottage is coming up for sale at the end of the holiday season," revealed Karen.

Nicki nodded. "I heard that too."

"Really," exclaimed Hetty, "it's a lovely place." She turned her head so as to look at Natalie while Karen removed a hair clip. "We stayed there last summer for a holiday. It's smashing. There's a gate at the bottom of the garden which leads onto a path and steps that go down to the beach."

"Sounds lovely but I should imagine it'll be way out of our price range."

"Luke Burleigh's mother was a Berryman! We ought to tell the police," spluttered Lottie, when Hetty arrived home and repeated what she'd heard in the hairdressers. "I mean, Natalie seems nice enough but I'm still not convinced about her husband and the police did say to let them know if anything else cropped up."

"I'm inclined to agree, but not yet. Let's wait a while and see what they find if and when Peter's body is exhumed."

Lottie groaned. "Ugh, I'd momentarily forgotten about that. I'm beginning to wish we'd not told the police of our theories."

Hetty shook her head. "They wouldn't do something like exhumation without good cause so I don't think we've any reason to feel guilty."

The wind freshened later in the afternoon and then just before six it began to rain; shortly after the first rumble of thunder, Hetty received a text from Grace asking if it would be alright if she came round with Malcolm and Belinda Jackson. Hetty said of course and then fetched the suitcase into the sitting room ready for their perusal.

Malcolm was thrilled to sift through the contents of the suitcase and to hear what had so far been learned about the Tregears and the Berrymans. While he was looking at the details Hetty had written on the lining paper pinned to the wall, Belinda picked up the wallet.

"Old money," she giggled, tipping the notes and coins into her lap, "I've never seen any of it before." She lifted up the one pound note. "It's beautiful and a ten shilling note too. What's that in today's money?"

"Fifty pence," laughed Lottie.

"Yes, of course, I remember now, there were twenty shillings in a pound back then."

"Oh, to be young enough to only know decimal currency," sighed Grace, "it makes me feel quite old."

"But I'm forty," Belinda divulged, "so not that young."

Before Belinda returned the money into the wallet, she ran her long slim fingers deep inside the pocket. "Ow, there's something else in here. More money notes perhaps."

"It can't be," insisted Hetty, "there were only two one pound notes and the ten bob note."

But to everyone's surprise Belinda pulled out a small photograph which had part slipped inside the lining. "A young lady," she cried, "and a pretty young lady at that." She crossed the room and gave the photograph to Hetty and Lottie who sat side by side on the settee.

"Hmm, how did we manage to miss finding this?" Hetty frowned.

Lottie put on her reading glasses. "It doesn't really matter. What's of more interest is, who is she?"

"Perhaps she's Polly," suggested Hetty, "you know, Simon Berryman's aunt."

"Hmm, intriguing," said Malcolm, pointing to the lining paper, "because according to this chart Polly was David Tregear's stepsister but perhaps there was more to the relationship than that."

"Wouldn't that be against the law?" Hetty asked.

Malcolm smiled. "No, step-siblings are not blood related so there is nothing to stop them having a relationship and marrying even. Be different if they were half brother and sister because then they would share a parent."

"Yes, of course, silly me."

Lottie scratched her head. "So if Polly was David's girlfriend, what does that have to do with him disappearing?"

"Well, it could be like we said the other day when we didn't know who the girlfriend was. Polly was probably someone else's girl and David stole her from him. The other chap, who we assume to be the hearse driver, found out, killed David in a fit of rage and hid his body in Peter's coffin." Hetty almost sounded convincing.

"Yes," agreed Lottie, "and then I suppose the bloke whoever he was would have started the rumour that David had run away to avoid conscription meaning Polly wouldn't have reason to wonder where he'd gone. Well, she might have wondered where but have no reason to question why."

"You make quite a good team of amateur sleuths," laughed Belinda, "I wish I had your vivid imaginations."

"Thank you," said Hetty, missing the fact that Belinda spoke with tongue-in-cheek.

Lottie frowned. "But we still don't know anything about the hearse driver. It's most frustrating," she tutted, "We don't even know his name."

"Unless it was old Jimmy," reasoned Hetty, thinking of the painting in her bedroom, "Although I don't really like the idea that the Old Jimmy in my picture was a bad person because he has a kindly face and sad eyes, but then do murderers ever look evil?"

Lottie twiddled her fingers. "Not very often and especially when the crime is not premeditated."

"Well whatever," smiled Grace, "it's all guess work and we don't even know that the lady in the photograph is Polly."

Lottie groaned. "That's the trouble. It is all guesswork and if I'm honest I don't think we're really any further forward today than we were when we first found the wretched suitcase."

"Sadly you're right," conceded Hetty, "and if we ever learn the truth and find that David was murdered, all I hope is that the deadly deed took place anywhere other than inside this house." As her words faded a sudden loud clap of thunder rattled through the building and brought Albert running in from his bed in the kitchen. He jumped up onto Hetty's lap and, whining and trembling, buried his face under her arm.

Chapter Thirteen

Thursday morning dawned bright and sunny and everywhere smelled fresh and clean after the overnight rain. In the back garden when she went to hang out the washing, Lottie found several apples had fallen prematurely from the tree in the wind. No flower stems were broken but the nibbled leaves on the dahlias and lupins was evidence that slugs and snails had enjoyed a midnight feast.

In the sitting room, Hetty gazed at the lining paper where she had pinned the small picture of the young lady they supposed might be Polly Berryman. As she picked up a pen to write Polly Berryman followed by a question mark beneath the photograph, she heard a car tooting outside. When she went to see who it was she found Vince Royale parking her car on the tarmac.

"Oh lovely, thank you," she cried, "I've missed the old car. Is everything alright now?"

"Yes, we've fixed the brakes and I've changed the oil as well so she should be fine."

"Would you like me to run you back to the garage?" Hetty asked seeing that he was alone.

"No, it's okay, one of the lads is picking me up. He should be here any minute."

Right on cue a truck appeared with Vince Royle's Garage written on the side along with his email address.

"Email address…internet," muttered Hetty, as the truck drove away, "Of course, why didn't I think of it before?"

She took a magnifying glass from a drawer in the kitchen and ran up the stairs to her room. From beside a chair she picked up the painting of Old Jimmy, sat down on the bed and placed it on her lap. Then using the magnifying glass she looked at the artist's signature to see if it was legible. It was faint but she was able to make out the name. It was S J Choak. Placing the painting back by the chair she went downstairs, switched on her laptop and typed S J Choak into the search box. To her delight the name came up amongst a list of Cornish artists. He was born in 1890 and died in 1967, but no other information was available.

Hetty was just about to tell Lottie what she had discovered, when the doorbell rang. On the doorstep was Sid.

"Taps," Sid held up a small box.

"Excellent," said Hetty, stepping aside, "come in."

As Sid stepped over the threshold he caught sight of the teddy bear on the stool in the corner of the sitting room. "Alright, Saff?" he chuckled, and gave the bear the thumbs up sign.

"I get the impression you like that little bear," smiled Hetty as she closed the front door.

"Yes, I do. There's something about his face that appeals. Having said that I like all bears but don't you go broadcasting that fact."

"I won't but I know what you mean and I agree."

Sid's smile vanished. "On a more sombre note. There were several people in the churchyard when I left home this morning and a white tent was being erected around the grave of Peter Tregear. I should imagine they've gone by now though."

Lottie groaned. "Oh dear. I do hope we've not sent the police on a wild goose chase. On the other hand I hope Peter was buried alone and that David wasn't murdered as we've suggested. I'd like to think the lad ran away and lived happily ever after."

"Well, time will tell because I shouldn't think they'd put the tent up if exhumation wasn't imminent." Sid held up the box, "Anyway, the wash basin taps are here at last and so I'll put them on and then I'll be finished."

"Wonderful," said Lottie, "Basil reckons he and Mark will finish today as well."

Grace arrived as Sid went upstairs with the taps so she and the sisters went outside to sit in the back garden.

"A penny for your thoughts," smiled Lottie to Grace who appeared to be looking into space. "You seem miles away."

Grace laughed. "I was just thinking how nice it would be to receive a letter from John. You know, a proper hand written letter delivered by the postman. It'd be nice to write one too. Such a shame that technology has superseded that art and I fear it will never return."

"I wholeheartedly agree. Emails and text messages just aren't the same even if they are quicker, free and save time."

"Exactly. I bought a postcard of Pentrillick yesterday and posted it to John this morning but it seemed rather futile because I've already sent him pictures on my phone and of course he can Google it anyway."

"I've some interesting news," interrupted Hetty, before Lottie and Grace could discuss further modes of communication. "The painting I bought of Old Jimmy was painted by a Cornish artist who was born in 1890 and died in 1967. So my Old Jimmy will almost certainly have been a Cornishman."

Lottie looked amazed. "Really?"

"Yes, so I'm pretty certain now, as much as it goes against the grain, that the chap in my painting is the Old Jimmy that Peter Tregear referred to on the postcard and that he may well be the hearse driver."

"Certainly food for thought," agreed Grace, although she didn't look convinced, "but even if it is it's still not possible to find out anything about him without a surname."

Hetty's shoulders slumped. "No, I suppose not."

"He doesn't really look like a hearse driver," reasoned Lottie, "he looks more like a fisherman even though he worked on a farm."

"But that's silly. Just because he has a moustache and a beard and is wearing a cap doesn't mean he wouldn't scrub-up well. Anyway, it was wartime and so there would have been a shortage of men."

"And," Grace added, "if the gentleman in Hetty's picture and the hearse driver-cum-farmworker were one and the same man then he would also have served on the lifeboat which might explain his nautical appearance."

"Thank you, Grace. I'm glad you can see reason."

Grace giggled. "You're welcome, Hetty but I have to admit I'm inclined to agree with Lottie and very much doubt that your Old Jimmy is in any way connected to the disappearance of David."

A little later when they went back indoors, they found a small package lying on the doormat.

"Oh look, the postman's been," Lottie bent down and picked up the padded envelope. She looked at the label. "Whatever can it be? It's addressed to both of us, but we're not expecting anything, are we, Het?"

"No, but you wanted some handwritten post and now you have it."

"Not quite the same as a letter though, is it?" Lottie shook it but it appeared not to rattle.

"I suppose it might be from Simon," suggested Hetty, "You never know, he might have decided to send on the old pictures rather than wait until they visit us."

"I doubt it. Anyway, I'll leave you to open it while I put the kettle on before we get complaints from the attic. Mustn't neglect them on their last day although I daresay Sid's finished already and is just chatting." Lottie handed the package to Hetty and went into the kitchen.

Grace and Hetty went into the sitting room to await their coffee and Hetty sat down to open the package. As she broke the seal there was a bang and a sudden flash. She screamed as the padded envelope caught fire. Grace leapt to her feet, quickly grabbed the burning package and tossed it onto the hearth. She then ran into the kitchen for a bowl of cold water and plunged Hetty's burnt hands into it.

"Oh my God," shrieked Lottie, who had followed Grace into the sitting room, "a letter bomb. Who on earth could have sent that?"

"I don't know," groaned Hetty, trembling but relieved to see the burns were not bad and she was more shaken than injured. She tried to laugh. "But I don't think I'll be wearing these trousers again. They're unrepairable even for you, Lottie."

Lottie gasped on seeing the large holes in her sister's trousers and the surrounding scorch marks. "I'm ringing the police," she cried, and dashed into the hallway where the number they had been given to ring was tucked behind a vase of flowers. As she picked up the phone, Sid, Basil and Mark rushed down the stairs to see who had screamed and why.

While they waited for the police, Grace dabbed Hetty's hands with bicarbonate of soda and wrapped them in gauze bandages.

"Looks to me like you need police protection," Basil stated, "How many attempts have there been on your lives now?"

"Just a couple," muttered Hetty, trying to trivialise the situation, "Today's effort and the car brakes. The phone calls were in no way a threat to our lives."

"Oh, I thought there was something else," Basil scowled as he tried to recall another incident.

"You're thinking of Simon Berryman being poisoned," voiced Lottie.

"Of course. How is he getting on?"

"Very well and he's due out of hospital today, thank goodness."

"Have you fitted the new taps, Sid?" Hetty asked, keen to change the subject.

Sid nodded. "Yes, they're all done so you can shower in there or whatever as soon as you want."

"And we've as good as finished too," chuckled Basil, "Just a bit of clearing up to do and then it'll all be yours."

Inside Pentrillick's churchyard, the badly decomposed coffin containing the remains of Peter Tregear was slowly and with reverence lifted from his grave onto the grass where the tarnished nameplate was checked to ratify the occupant was indeed Peter Tregear. His coffin was then lowered into a fibreglass shell, the lid screwed down and a nameplate with his name and the date of his demise attached to the exterior lid.

Kitty Thomas who played the church organ, was walking along the main street of the village when the vehicles left the graveyard. As they drove by she lowered her head and said a little prayer.

Chapter Fourteen

On Monday, Kyle had the whole day off work and so in the morning he drove Zac and Emma to Penzance to get white matt paint for the three of them had volunteered to paint the walls of the new bedrooms.

Ten minutes after they had left, Hetty and Lottie had a visit from the police who informed them that Peter Tregear was buried alone and that the remains were definitely him because there was evidence of the injuries he had received during the war as ratified by his military records. They also learned that Peter had died in a British hospital having been shipped home from abroad because his injuries were life threatening and it was unlikely that he would ever be able to be part of active service again.

"That lets Luke Burleigh off the hook then," sighed Hetty, as the police car drove away, "Well, his family at least."

"His family name," corrected Lottie, "After all we've no reason at all to suppose Luke is related to the Berrymans we're interested in."

Hetty looked dejected. "And I suppose it lets Old Jimmy off the hook too. Although in a way I'm glad about that because I've got to like him. As I said the other day he has a kindly face and sad eyes."

Lottie laughed. "Oh, come on, Het. You must have known all along that the chances of your Old Jimmy in the painting and the hearse driver being the same man were very, very slim."

"But Old Jimmy might still be the hearse driver. It's just we know now that he didn't kill David. Having said that he might have murdered him but obviously not in the manner we'd imagined, who knows?"

"Well not us, that's for sure."

"You're right but my instincts tell me there is a link there somewhere. Meanwhile we've come up against yet another brick wall and our investigations into the disappearance of poor old David are now right back to square one."

"Yes they are, but the answer must still be within our grasp otherwise why would our lives have been threatened several times this summer? I mean we weren't threatened in any way before we found the suitcase, were we? So its discovery has to be the reason for our um…accidents."

"Perhaps by opening up the suitcase we unleashed a curse." Hetty spoke with tongue firmly in cheek.

"Hmm, and pigs might fly."

"But then again we mustn't forget the Scrabble message. I mean it's more than likely that someone does have skeletons in their closet over all this."

Lottie laughed. "Don't let's go down that path again. Yes, someone may well be hiding something but to suggest some unknown spirit or whatever warned us in a game of Scrabble is far too silly."

Hetty stood up and fetched her walking shoes from the cupboard under the stairs. "Okay. Anyway, I'm tired of thinking about it and so I'm going to take Albert out for a walk. Do you fancy coming with me?"

"Where are you planning to go?"

"I thought along the clifftop in an easterly direction as the weather's looking good. The wind's light as well so it should be very pleasant."

"I'll come then. I could do with some good clean sea air to clear my head. I must admit thinking about David's plight is giving me a headache."

"Me too and if you come you can hold Albert's lead because my hands are still feeling a bit sore."

They left Primrose Cottage with Albert on his lead. As they passed the gates of Tuzzy-Muzzy, Lottie paused. "Do you think we ought to ask Grace if she'd like to join us?"

"She's not here today," Hetty answered without stopping, "She made an appointment to have her hair coloured this morning after I sang the praises of Karen and Nicki."

Lottie fell into step beside her sister. "Of course, silly me."

They joined the coastal path by access of a track on the opposite side of the road to the Pentrillick Hotel.

"If only walls could talk," mused Lottie, glancing up at the grand looking hotel, "it'd save us so much trouble."

"Maybe," agreed Hetty, "but I reckon the walls of our own house might be able to tell us more than those of the hotel."

"Yes, you've made a good point there."

A light south easterly breeze blew warm air onto their faces as they walked away from Pentrillick and followed the well-worn path between clumps of bracken, gorse and the occasional patch of colourful wild mesembryanthemums. Above, the rich blue sky stretched for miles unbroken by even one wispy white cloud, and below, the clear water of the turquoise sea showed glimpses of rock beneath the surface of the gently rippling waves. Ships and large vessels seemed motionless on the distant horizon while near to the shore, anglers clutched their fishing rods in a small boat as it chugged along the rugged coastline.

The sisters followed the meandering path neither speaking, but instead enjoying the peace and quiet. Even gulls flying in circles overhead seemed keen not to break the tranquillity of the glorious day.

After the path ran down a slight incline, Hetty stopped and pointed to a small cove below where a granite building lay nestled between the rocks. "The Old Lifeboat House. I'd forgotten we'd be passing that by coming this way."

"Me too," Lottie paused and stood beside her sister. "I wish we could go and have a closer look as I'd love to see what it's used for now."

"Hmm, probably still a studio for someone or other."

As she spoke, a woman appeared round the side of the building carrying two large, bulky, black bin liners which she placed beside a parked car. When she saw Hetty and Lottie, she waved.

"That's Tess Dobson," gasped Hetty, shading her eyes from the sunlight.

Lottie didn't look convinced. "Are you sure?"

"Well, that's her car."

The woman beckoned the sisters towards her.

"Come on," urged Hetty, pulling down the sleeves of her cardigan to cover her hands and hide the bandages, "we might be able to do some exploring."

"I knew it was you when I saw Albert," grinned Tess, as she bent forwards and stroked the dog's soft warm head, "and had to call you down to see if you'd had any luck with your investigations?"

Hetty wrinkled her nose. "So, so."

"Which means not really," Lottie added. "We've not found out what happened to David anyway. We just seem to come up against one brick wall after another."

"Oh, that's a shame."

"But we'll not give up," Hetty emphasised as she attempted to peep through the Old Lifeboat House window.

"Would you like a look round?" Tess asked, having no doubt as to what the answer would be. "There'll be no-one here until tomorrow."

"We'd love to," Hetty hastily replied, "but what is it used for now?"

"It's a holiday let and has been since May. Come on, I'll show you round."

They entered the building by a side door flanked by large terracotta pots containing pelargoniums, trailing lobelia and begonias.

"So are you the housekeeper?" Lottie asked as she gazed around the brightly lit interior.

"Yes, and I love coming out here. It's the favourite of all my little jobs. It's so peaceful and for a few hours I like to pretend I live here."

The downstairs was open plan with kitchen and dining areas towards the back and a sitting area at the front with breath-taking views of the sea.

"Does it get battered much by the sea in winter?" Hetty asked, looking from the large triple glazed window onto the slipway below.

"If the wind is in the southeast, yes. But the prevailing wind in Cornwall is from the southwest so it doesn't fare too badly."

Lottie pointed up towards the mezzanine floor. "I assume up there are the bedrooms."

"That's right. There are two of them, a double and a twin. Come and take a peep."

Lining the wall of the staircase were several framed black and white pictures of men standing alongside their lifeboats.

Hetty gasped. "Are these pictures of the Pentrillick lifeboat crews?"

"Yes, although I doubt if everyone who ever served on the lifeboat is here."

"Are there any from the 1940s?" Hetty eagerly asked.

"Two," Tess pointed to the pictures in question, "this one was taken in 1941 and the other in 1949 just before the boathouse was closed down."

Lottie gasped. "Wow, do you think David might be on one of them, Het?"

"That's what I'm hoping. The trouble is I didn't bring my reading specs with me. Did you, Lottie?"

Lottie shook her head.

"Damn."

"Do you have a phone with you?" Tess asked.

Hetty nodded. "I never go anywhere without it as you never know when it might be needed."

"Then take a photo of the photo," suggested Tess, "then when you get home you can zoom in on it to get a better look."

"Good thinking," Hetty eagerly fumbled in the large pocket of her cardigan for her phone. She then took several photos of the 1941 picture but only two of the 1949 as they knew by then David was already missing.

"We'll study these closely when we get back," said Hetty excitedly as she tucked the phone back into her pocket. "We know what David looks like because there was a picture of him with Peter in our attic."

Lottie shared her sister's enthusiasm. "It'll be interesting to see what his fellow lifeboat men were like and one of them might even be the mystery man who drove the hearse for the Berrymans."

"Oh, how I wish these chaps could speak to us," sighed Hetty, as she waved her hand at the pictures, "they would be able to answer so many of our questions."

Tess folded her arms. "Well someone around here today must know something or you wouldn't keep getting strange things happen to you. I heard that someone had tampered with the brakes on your car the other day and it's common knowledge that Simon Berryman was poisoned while visiting the area."

"And don't forget the letter bomb," Lottie added.

Tess's jaw dropped. "A letter bomb."

Lottie grimaced. "Damn, we agreed not to let anyone know about that."

"I won't say a word," muttered Tess.

"Really," chuckled Hetty.

Tess's shoulders slumped. "Well, I'll try not to."

"Oh, it doesn't matter," laughed Hetty, noting the look of disappointment on Tess's face, "tell who you want. It won't really make any difference, and Sid, Basil and Mark know anyway because they were there when we received it."

"And Grace," Lottie added.

"Yes, of course. Grace too."

"So what exactly happened?"

Tess listened intently while the sisters told of the morning the letter bomb had arrived with the post.

When they arrived back at Primrose Cottage, Kyle's van was parked by the garage and upstairs he along with Zac and Emma were busy painting the walls and ceilings of one of the new bedrooms.

"My goodness, you don't waste any time," said Hetty, seeing that the larger of the two rooms was nearly finished.

"Rollers are so quick. We'd still have a long way to go if we'd used brushes." Zac lifted the ten litre tub and poured more paint into the tray.

Hetty shook her head. "I don't get on with rollers. The only time I ever used one there was more paint on me than on the wall and as for using them for ceilings…it'd be impossible although I see you've managed alright."

Lottie nodded. "Same here. It must be an age thing."

"Or we don't have the knack."

"Is that the phone I can hear?" Emma asked.

Lottie put her head round the door. "Yes, it is," she then went downstairs and Hetty followed.

When Lottie answered the phone there was no-one there.

"Here we go again," she snapped and slammed down the receiver.

In all they received another three calls and all within a space of fifteen minutes. As before the fourth ended with heavy breathing and then a scream. However, to the surprise of the sisters, the police came round soon after. They had traced the calls to the old red phone box in the village.

In the evening Hetty plugged her phone into her laptop so that they could look at the pictures of the lifeboat men. In the 1941 photograph the crew were wearing life jackets, sea boots and flat caps. The 1949 crew wore long mackintoshes and sou'westers.

"There's David," Lottie pointed to the young man second from the left.

"Well spotted. I wonder if my Old Jimmy the hearse driver is on this too. I'm quite familiar with his looks now."

Lottie tutted but said nothing.

Hetty picked up a magnifying glass and looked at the picture in more detail. "Oh no," she laughed, as the magnifying glass scanned the bow of the boat, "Oh no. Oh dear. You're never going to believe this, Lottie. You see Old Jimmy *is* on the picture but there's no way he's the hearse driver. Old Jimmy is the lifeboat."

Chapter Fifteen

Seeing the Goliath brought a lump to Hetty's throat. Much of the wood had rotted leaving gaping holes. Where paint was still visible it had flaked and faded but the name on the stern was as clear as the day the boat was new.

"Do you think you'll ever restore it?" Lottie asked Tristan Liddicott-Treen. "I know it was your father's project and he's no longer with us but it seems such a shame to let it deteriorate further."

"I whole heartedly agree," replied Justin, rubbing his hand along the gunwales, "especially since you've told me about the suitcase in your attic. To be honest, woodwork isn't a skill I possess but I know a man who is extremely talented and so I shall ask him to restore it for me."

"That's cheered me no-end," said Hetty, "Thank you."

"It's the least I can do and perhaps when it is fully restored and seaworthy I can take you ladies out for trip along the coast."

"Wow," gushed Lottie, "that would be wonderful. I'd love to see Pentrillick from off-shore."

Hetty and Lottie along with Grace were in one of the outbuildings in the grounds of Pentrillick House viewing the boat following its discovery by Bernie the Boatman. Afterwards, they wandered down to the café and while sitting by the lake drinking coffee, Luke Burleigh walked by, hands in pockets, whistling a tune not at all familiar to the three ladies.

"Does that chap not like you two?" Grace asked, a puzzled look on her face.

"Humph," snorted Hetty.

Lottie smiled, amused by her sister's taciturn response. "Let's put it like this, we don't exactly see eye to eye but what makes you ask that, Grace?"

"Well, it's just he was glaring at you in the pub the other night which I thought was a little strange."

"Was he?" Lottie pulled a face.

"He's probably heard on the grapevine that we've been asking questions about him," growled Hetty, watching Luke until he was out of sight.

Lottie laughed. "Well it was hardly on the grapevine, Het. It was his wife you were grilling and she no doubt told him."

"So who is he then?" Grace asked.

"Luke Burleigh," growled Hetty, "he lives a few doors away from us in Blackberry Way at Fuchsia Cottage. He's renting it from Tommy Thomas because Tom hasn't lived there now since he married Kitty and moved into Meadowsweet with her."

"Meadowsweet is where Kitty already lives and has done for donkey's years," Lottie added to put Grace in the picture.

"I see. So what does this Luke chappie do?" Grace asked.

"Apparently he's a science teacher," scoffed Hetty, "He's not been in the area long and comes from Rochdale."

"And his mother's maiden name was Berryman," Lottie added, "but she's not one of the Cornish Berrymans from down here."

"His mother was a Berryman and he's a science teacher," gasped Grace, "Oh my goodness me."

Hetty frowned. "Why has your face gone all pink?"

"Has it?" Grace touched her rosy cheeks.

"I just told you he's not related to our Berrymans," said Lottie, emphatically, "so there's nothing to get excited about. And we know it's true because Het asked his wife, Natalie, didn't you, Het?"

"Yes, when I was at the hairdressers."

"Humph, well I reckon he's up to no good," blurted Grace. Her brows tightly knitted.

A vacant look crossed the faces of both Hetty and Lottie.

"Explain," demanded Lottie.

"Well, you tell me he's a Berryman and he's also a science teacher."

"That's right, but so what?" Lottie drained her coffee mug and placed it by her feet.

"Well, if you take his occupation and his name and mix the two, then I'd say you have a pretty lethal combination."

"What on earth are you on about?" Hetty was clearly baffled.

"Mumbo jumbo," snapped Lottie.

"Oh come on, use your brains, girls," spluttered Grace, "I'm referring to the letter bomb. It must have been made by someone with a little or a lot of scientific knowledge. I mean most people wouldn't have a clue about explosives, would they?"

"Good point," Lottie agreed, "but surely such things can be Googled, meaning anyone could have done it."

Hetty's jaw dropped. "No, Lottie. I think Grace has hit the nail on the head. I'm going to ring the police as soon as we get home. I think surely Burleigh has some explaining to do."

"I hear young Luke Burleigh has been questioned by the police regarding the letter bomb you received," chided Kitty, when she and Tommy called round in the evening with some tomatoes grown in their greenhouse.

"Oh, they do look nice, thank you," said Hetty, "but how do you know about Luke?"

"Because he told us," Kitty replied, "We just dropped some tomatoes in to him and Natalie as well. I'm not sure whether he was amused by the incident or cross. I find him difficult to make out."

"I hope he was amused," squeaked Lottie.

Hetty scowled. "I hope he was cross."

Kitty tutted. "Don't be like that, Hetty. I think they're a lovely young couple."

"Okay, so did he say anything about the police interview?"

"Only that he'd laughed when they asked about a letter bomb. Apparently he teaches natural science. You know biology and stuff, so explosives and suchlike aren't his thing."

"But his mother *was* a Berryman," gabbled Hetty.

"Yes, but he's done a bit of family history and so could prove that his mother has no connection with Cornwall whatsoever."

Lottie bit her bottom lip. "Oh dear, I think we must avoid him for a while."

"We'll blame Grace," chuckled Hetty, conscious that her face had warmed up, "she's the one that suggested he might be responsible for the letter bomb."

"Hmm, we will, but sadly if Luke is in the clear we're back to square one yet again," muttered Lottie.

Hetty laughed. "Yes, once again we're face to face with the old brick wall."

"Perhaps David Tregear had an accident," suggested Tommy, as they all went into the sitting room and sat down, "you know, he fell down a mineshaft or something like that. There are lots of them about and back in the nineteen forties I daresay health and safety wasn't as stringent as it is today."

"But if that's the case why were his things hidden in our attic?" Lottie asked.

"Perhaps someone hid them to soften the blow to his mother," reasoned Kitty, "his stepbrother, George perhaps. After all if he had cause to believe that David had had an accident then he might have thought it better to suggest he'd run away rather than have her know or believe something horrible had happened to him."

Tommy nodded. "Yes, good point, Kitty. And it's worth remembering that with some of these mines it'd be difficult to retrieve a body especially during wartime when resources were stretched."

"Well if an accident such as you've suggested happened, Tommy, then someone must have been with him. Because if he'd been alone then no-one would've known about it, would they? Meaning, that if no-one knew there would have been no-one to cover up his disappearance by hiding his belongings." Hetty frowned, "I hope that makes sense."

"It does, and if so it's likely the person in question would have been too afraid to tell anyone because he or she hadn't been able to save the poor chap and therefore felt guilty." Tommy spoke with conviction.

Hetty scowled. "But that someone would have needed to have told George in order for George to have hidden the suitcase in our attic."

"Either George or the hearse driver who lodged here," reasoned Lottie.

Hetty sighed. "Okay, so for the sake of argument let's assume David fell down a mineshaft. Who then might have been with him to have witnessed his fall?"

Lottie glanced at the lining paper pinned to the wall. "Perhaps it was the girlfriend."

"But I thought you were only guessing that he had a girlfriend," teased Kitty.

"Yes, we were." Lottie looked at her sister. "Why are you scowling, Het?"

"Oh, was I? I didn't realise. But I was just thinking about Polly, you having mentioned a girlfriend. You see, what's suddenly occurred to me is why she wasn't called up during the war? I mean women of her age were, weren't they? After all she had no children and she didn't work in any of the categories that were exempt."

"Good point," Kitty agreed, "perhaps it might be worth asking Simon when next you see him. Although I doubt that he'll know. If I'm honest I've no idea what my aunts and uncles did during the war."

"And whatever her reason for avoiding conscription doesn't help us solve the David mystery anyway," said Lottie.

"I agree and going back to what we were saying a few minutes ago, I don't think David had an accident at all simply because if he had then why is someone trying to harm Lottie and me? Not to mention poor Simon. What's more, I'm sure George wouldn't have tried to deceive his stepmother like that. Remember George was Simon's father and I think Simon is as straight as a die."

Lottie nodded. "Yes, you're right and I agree. What's more I think it might be time we accepted that we'll never know the truth and we can hypothesise 'til the cows come home."

"You want to give up?" Hetty was flabbergasted.

"Well, unless we get a few more clues I don't think we have a choice."

"I shall never give up even if it takes me the rest of my life. Anyway, something will turn up soon, I feel it in my bones."

Chapter Sixteen

On Friday morning, Hetty and Lottie drove down to Penzance to look at bedroom furniture for the new rooms. Lottie also wanted to buy fabric to make curtains for the windows even though Hetty said it would be much easier to buy some readymade. The shopping trip was a success. They found furniture they liked and placed an order. After finding fabric to her liking, Lottie bought the amount that would be needed. They also bought a huge box of chocolates which they knew to be Grace's favourites.

In the evening, Grace took Hetty, Lottie and Zac out for a meal at the Crown and Anchor to celebrate her fifty-ninth birthday. They had a large table booked in the dining room because she had also invited along several young people with whom Zac was friends, including Emma and Kyle. Tommy and Kitty and Alex and Ginny and the Jacksons were also guests.

After the meal, the party returned to the bar; the youngsters went into the games area to play pool and the rest went and sat outside but there was very little warmth. The evening sun had moved round plunging the whole terrace into shade so, after they finished their drinks they decided it was too chilly to remain outdoors and went back inside.

Sitting at the bar, Lottie observed a man who had looked in their direction on several occasions since they had come in from outside. He was talking to the garage proprietor, Vince Royale and when he caught Lottie's eye, he left his bar stool and approached the party.

"I'm sorry to interrupt your gathering but I wonder if you'll permit me to meet up with you some time. The man leaning on the bar told me that you're the people I'm looking for. It's about the suitcase you found in your attic, you see."

All ears pricked up.

"How come you know about the suitcase?" Kitty asked, knowing the young man was not a local.

"My girlfriend told me. She started work at the Pentrillick Hotel last week and heard all about it there."

"Really!" Hetty exclaimed, "Are you able to tell us what happened to David Tregear then by any chance?"

"Sadly, not. But in the past I've spoken with someone who knew the Tregear family well." He smiled broadly, "That person being my grandmother, Edith Triggs."

Lottie gasped. "Is your grandmother still alive? Please tell me she is."

The young man shook his head. "Regrettably not and if she was she'd be one hundred years old now."

"Oh, what a shame, but if you've something to tell us, why can't you tell us now?" Hetty was eager to hear what the young man had to say.

"Because it's a bit noisy in here and I'm going in a minute. My girlfriend is picking me up on her way home from work." He handed Lottie a card. "Ring me when it's convenient and I'll come and see you. I'm self-employed and so my time is my own."

His phone beeped. "Must go, Angie's waiting. Nice to have met you and I look forward to seeing you again."

"Well, what do you make of that?" Hetty asked, as the young man dashed out of the building.

"Sounds promising," said Lottie, as she looked at the card. "According to this his name is Steve Martin and he's a freelance journalist."

"Hmm, probably just after a story then," scoffed Grace, dismissively, "and he's made up the grandmother business to get your attention."

"Ow, I don't think so," said Lottie, "I thought him very sincere."

"What did he say his grandmother's name was?" Ginny asked.

"Edith Triggs," Alex replied, "and when we get home I'll have a look at the list of people who attended Peter Tregear's funeral to see if she's amongst them."

"Excellent idea," agreed Hetty, rubbing her hands together, "and if she is then we'll definitely give Steve Martin a ring."

As they were leaving the Crown and Anchor, Lottie spotted on the floor one of the small business cards which Bernie the Boatman handed out to potential customers telling of his fishing trips. She bent down to pick it up and when she turned it over saw a name written on the back. "Anne Smith." She frowned, "Why does that name ring a bell?"

Grace peered over Lottie's shoulder. "My mother was Anne Smith."

"How peculiar," blurted Hetty, "I wonder why her name's written on Bernie's card?"

Alex laughed. "Well, with all due respect to Grace, Hetty, I think it's highly unlikely that Grace's mother is the only person to have ever been given that name."

"True," laughed Grace, "it never ceases to amaze me when I'm looking for an old friend on Facebook and type in a name in the search box just how many people there are with the same name and I'm talking about names much less common than that of my dear old mum."

Chapter Seventeen

The following morning, Alex called in on his way to the antique shop. He had checked the list of mourners at Peter Tregear's funeral and Edith Triggs was amongst them.

"Brilliant," shrieked Hetty, clapping her hands with glee, "we're getting somewhere at last. We'll ring Steve Martin straight away. It should be interesting to hear what he has to tell us even though he doesn't appear to know what happened to David."

"Absolutely and if by any chance he's able to visit tomorrow then I'd love to hear what he has to say as well, if that's alright with you."

"Of course, Alex, you'd be most welcome. Without you and your research we'd probably have got no further than reading gravestones."

Lottie rang Steve Martin as soon as Alex left and he agreed to visit them the following afternoon.

"So what shall we do today?" Hetty asked.

"How about going to the garden centre and buying some plants for the pond?" Lottie proposed, "I think the water's had enough time to settle by now."

"But isn't it supposed to be left for several weeks?"

"That's only if we're putting fish in. We've not discussed it yet but shall we have fish eventually?"

"It would be nice as long as herons don't pinch them."

"Do you think they might?"

"Yes, definitely. I was talking to Chloe the other day and she knows someone who lost all their fish last winter and so they now have a large plastic heron by their pond. Chloe said they're going to get one for their pond too before winter in case the same thing happens to them."

Hetty and Lottie were unloading the car after the trip to the garden centre when Grace called. "Excellent, plants for the pond. Are you going to put them in now?"

"No time like the present," Hetty lifted up a bag of aquatic compost and stood it on the ground, "Would you like to give us a hand?"

"You bet," Grace eagerly stepped forward and took a pot containing a waterlily from the back of the car along with several aquatic baskets in varying sizes.

After they had carried everything round to the back garden they potted all the new plants up in the baskets and then steadily positioned them in the water. A yellow iris, water forget-me-nots, a marsh marigold and an umbrella plant were placed on the marginal shelf and oxygenating plants were dropped onto the surface with weights to pull them down. To enable them to get the water lily in the middle of the pond where the water was deepest, Hetty changed into her swimming costume and waded in.

"The water is actually quite warm. I'm surprised."

"Hmm, but I don't think I'll join you," Lottie turned to go indoors. "I'll make tea instead."

When Lottie came back out with the tea tray and a large towel draped over her arm, Hetty was out of the pond and sitting on the bench with Grace, both admiring their handiwork. Lottie threw Hetty the towel. "I thought you might want to dry your legs."

"Thanks." Hetty stood up and wrapped the towel around the lower part of her body.

"Grace and I were just saying we must have a pond-warming party now the pond is done. What do you think, Lottie?"

Lottie sat down. "I think it's a lovely idea and we must have it before Zac goes home. It can be a pond-warming, farewell do."

"Good, when we go in we'll check the calendar and choose a date."

"Have you told Grace about Steve Martin yet?" Lottie asked.

"Oh no, I'd completely forgotten," Hetty turned to Grace. "Steve Martin, you know the chap we saw in the pub last night, well he's coming here tomorrow to see us. I hope you can make it."

"Oh dear but no I can't which is a shame because I should really like to hear what he has to say. You see, I've already agreed to go out for the day with the Jacksons tomorrow. They're going to the Eden Project and asked me if I'd like to join them as I'm interested in plants. And I don't want to let them down as they're going home on Monday."

"Oh well, never mind," sighed Lottie, "we can tell you all about it when you get back."

"Meanwhile we must sit patiently and wait for a dragonfly," laughed Hetty, "I see you're wearing your lovely brooch, Grace so hopefully it might attract one and it'll come and rest on your shoulder."

"Oh, I don't think I'd like the idea of one landing on me," scowled Lottie, "I know they're pretty but I like to keep all creepy-crawlies at arm's length."

Grace tutted. "My dear, Lottie, it's reckoned that if a dragonfly lands on you it will bring you good luck."

"Really," Hetty was intrigued.

Grace nodded. "Yes, and apparently if you see a dragonfly in your dreams or if one suddenly appears in your life, then that's a sign that you need to take care because something in your life is hidden and the truth is being kept from you."

"Hetty threw back her head and laughed. "Well, the truth regarding David Tregear is certainly being kept from us regardless of whether or not we'll see a dragonfly."

Chapter Eighteen

Steve Martin arrived promptly at Primrose Cottage on Sunday afternoon. Lottie showed him into the sitting room and introduced him to Hetty, Zac and Emma, Kitty and Tommy, Alex and Ginny and herself, most of whom he had seen on Friday evening. While Zac and Emma went into the kitchen to make tea for everyone, Simon and Sheila arrived.

"I hope we're not too late," Simon kissed Hetty and Lottie on the cheek in turn, "We got stuck behind a tractor for a mile or so."

Lottie smiled. "No, we've not started talking yet."

"Are you completely better?" Hetty asked, "I must admit you look fine."

"And I feel it," laughed Simon, "In fact I've never felt better."

"Good,"

As Hetty introduced Simon and Sheila to Steve Martin, Emma and Zac carried in mugs of tea and slices of cake on trays.

"I've brought the photos with me," Simon remarked, after shaking Steve's hand, "I'll show you them later when I've had a cup of tea because stupidly I've left them in the car."

"Plenty of time," insisted Lottie, taking a seat on the settee beside Hetty.

As Simon sat he cast his eyes around the room. When his eyes fell on Kitty a puzzled look crossed his face and then he gasped. "Kitty Kat," he whispered. She smiled as he put his mug down on the table, sprang to his feet and crossed the room. She stood up and to her surprise he flung his arms around her and hugged her tightly. "Kitty Kat, my first real friend. I've often wondered about you."

"And I you," murmured Kitty, "although I'm surprised you recognised me after all this time."

"It's the eyes," teased Simon, "I'd recognise those eyes anywhere. And of course I knew you still lived along here and were friends with our hostesses. What's more, I hear you're married now."

"Yes, and this is my husband, Tommy." She waved her hand to Tommy sitting by her empty chair."

The two men shook hands and then Simon beckoned Sheila to his side and introduced her to Kitty and Tommy.

"We'd forgotten you'd not met again yet," tutted Hetty, "how remiss of us."

Simon laughed. "Well my last visit did come to rather an abrupt end."

"Yes," mumbled Sheila, "and let's hope this time things are a little more run-of-the-mill."

Once the chatter lessened they all took their seats again.

"Sorry about the interruption, Steve," apologised Hetty, "When you're ready we're all longing to hear what you have to tell us and then afterwards I'll go and fetch the suitcase so you can rootle through it."

"Well, I hope you won't be disappointed." He finished off his slice of cake and put the empty plate down on the coffee table; he then opened up a brown envelope. "I have here some pictures of my grandmother, Edith Triggs, and also one of David Tregear." He handed the pictures to Hetty to pass around. "You see, my grandmother was David Tregear's girlfriend and they planned to marry after the war ended. Of course that never happened and to say Grandma was mystified by David's disappearance would be an understatement."

"Sorry to interrupt," apologised Hetty, as she rose and crossed to the lining paper pinned to the wall, "but having seen that photo of your grandmother I realise she's the young lady in the picture that Belinda found in David's wallet who we assumed to be Polly." She took down the small photograph from the wall and handed it to Steve.

"Yes, that's Grandma. But who is Belinda?"

"Just someone staying in the guest house next door," explained Lottie, "We showed the suitcase to her and her husband because they were interested."

Steve nodded. "I see...I think."

"And at least we know it's not Polly now," acknowledged Hetty.

"Aunt Polly, you thought it was Aunt Polly," Simon stood and crossed the room to look at the small picture. He smiled. "No this young lady's nothing like Aunt Polly because she has fair hair. Aunt Polly was a brunette. She also had a larger frame. I know I was only young when I knew her but she was quite a bit taller than my mother and stouter too, although she must have been slimmer during wartime when food was rationed."

"I'm sorry, Steve," apologised Hetty, worried he might be annoyed, "I've caused us all to go off at a tangent. Please continue."

"Not a problem," laughed Steve, who was amused by the deviation. "Anyway, as I said Grandma was mystified by David's disappearance and for that reason she desperately tried to find out where he'd gone but sadly she just kept coming up at one brick wall after another."

Lottie laughed. "The old brick wall again. The times we've used that analogy in the last few weeks is no-one's business."

Hetty tutted, raised her forefinger to her lips and shushed her sister.

"Sorry," whispered Lottie.

"It's alright," said Steve, "It's nice to know you're listening. Now where was I?"

"Your grandmother kept coming up against brick walls," prompted Zac.

"That's right, she did, but she said she always felt that David's stepsister, Polly Berryman, who I now realise is your aunt, Simon, knew more than she'd admit. And I don't know whether you're aware of this, Simon, and I hope you won't be offended, but according to Grandma, Polly liked a drink. Gin was her tipple and she drank far more of it than was good for her and apparently got addicted to the stuff while running the hotel bar."

Simon looked shocked. "Good heavens that's news to me but then I only knew Aunt Polly for a few years and I was very young. It probably explains why Dad lost touch with her though because he was very much against drinking in excess."

Ginny tilted her head to one side. "Please excuse my ignorance. But was alcohol rationed during the war?"

"No it wasn't but the price increased dramatically as the war dragged on and in some places it was in short supply," answered Alex.

Hetty looked thoughtful as she addressed Steve. "So reading between the lines, would I be right in thinking that your grandmother and Polly didn't get on very well?"

Steve winkled his nose. "I must admit I did get that feeling when Grandma spoke of Polly and I don't suppose it helped that Grandma was tee-total, had a sharp tongue and called a spade a spade." Steve chuckled, "If the truth be known Grandma probably criticised poor Polly which would explain why one day Polly told Grandma that David had no doubt run away to get away from her nagging tongue."

Emma giggled.

Simon sat up straight. "So do you think it's possible he might have gone for that reason?"

"No, no, I don't think so for one minute," grinned Steve, "and I say that because Grandma told me so. Besides, he had too much to lose. He loved the railway, loved fishing and he was devoted to the lifeboat. What's more, he was devastated by the death of his brother, Peter, and would never have left his mother to whom he was devoted, to grieve alone."

"And if he went where would he go?" Sheila added, "With food rationed and so forth without an identity card and his ration book he would soon have starved to death."

"I wonder what happened to his ration book," said Alex, "I mean it wasn't in the suitcase, was it?"

Hetty tutted. "No, it wasn't. Strange. I wonder if someone found it and used it."

"Interesting point," agreed Steve, "Anyway, going back to Grandma and what Polly said, Grandma knew he would never have left her willingly simply because he loved her. Of that she had no doubt." Steve put his hand inside the brown envelope and pulled out a small box and a piece of paper. "I found out all I'm telling you about ten years ago when I asked Grandma about the family. I was trying to piece together family history, you see, having been inspired by the television programme, *Who Do You Think You Are*, and as Grandma was the oldest family member still living, she was the obvious person to question first." He held up the sheet of paper, "This is a poem David wrote for Grandma telling of his love for her and in this box is the engagement ring he gave to her on St. Valentine's Day in 1941." He handed the sheet of paper to Lottie; the ring he passed to Hetty.

Simon stood up. "Seeing your envelope has reminded me of my old photos. I'll just pop out to the car and get them."

"Did your grandmother ever mention a man who was a lodger here?" Sheila suddenly asked.

"What in this house?" Steve looked puzzled.

"Yes."

"I don't think she did. In fact I'm sure she didn't. Who was he?"

"That's what we'd all like to know," laughed Lottie, as she unfolded the sheet of paper Steve had given to her, "All we know is that he lodged here with George, worked on a farm, was crew on the lifeboat and drove the hearse for the Berrymans but because we don't know his name we've not been able to find out anything about him."

"For a while we thought he might have been called Jimmy though," laughed Hetty, "but now we know he wasn't because Jimmy's a boat. In fact Old Jimmy's a lifeboat or at least he was. Or should I say she, because apparently boats are ladies even when they have chaps' names."

Steve looked nonplussed.

Lottie tutted. "Shush, Het, you're just confusing matters."

Steve chuckled. "Oh dear, how frustrating for you. I wish I could help but the farm working, hearse driving, lifeboat lodger is news to me."

Hetty sighed as she opened the box and saw the ring. "Oh dear, it's all very sad and we're still none the wiser as to where David went but whatever happened it's nice to know that he had a girlfriend who loved and missed him."

Lottie nodded. "I agree, and one thing is for certain: that being, David did not run away." She handed the poem to her sister. "These verses are beautiful, Het and are not the sentiments of a rogue."

As Hetty read the poem, Simon returned with a plastic wallet. He tipped the old photographs out onto the coffee table. "Sadly these won't be any help either. All are of the Berrymans and most are of my parents, George and Betty. There is one of my grandfather though and just one of Aunt Polly, but none are very good and they're all far too small really to see any features."

"If only photography back then was as it is today," Lottie sighed. "I'd love to know what they all looked like. Not that that would help us much."

"I assume," said Kitty, addressing Steve, "that your grandmother eventually met someone else and married."

"Yes, she met and married Jeff Martin, who was of course my grandfather and they had fifty happy years together." As Steve's words faded his eyes became transfixed on something across the room.

"Are you alright," Lottie asked, aware that the colour had drained from Steve's face.

"That bear," Steve stood up and pointed to the spot where his eyes were focused, "Did he belong to David?"

Zac picked up the bear from his stool in the corner. "Yes, he was in the attic along with the rest of his stuff." He gave the bear to Steve.

"He wasn't in the suitcase though," added Lottie, "he was inside an old pillowslip."

Hetty was puzzled. "So how come you know about him?"

"Amongst Grandma's pictures is one of her holding a bear. I didn't bring it with me because it's a bit blurred." He stroked the top of the bear's head. "This must be him though because he has the same sad face and is wearing the same thin tie round his neck. If I remember correctly, the bear was a birthday present to David from his father."

Simon nodded. "That's right, David and Peter were both given a bear by their father on their third birthdays. I have Peter's bear. He's just the same as this little chap only he has a blue tie."

"Do you by any chance know his name?" Hetty asked Steve. "Several of us have had a guess but it'd be nice to know his real name so that we can stop referring to him as the bear."

"I suggested Pilchard," laughed Lottie, "because they were plentiful back then."

Hetty groaned. "My guess was Fred so not very imaginative."

"Because of the message on the postcard I went for Jimmy," said Zac, "but of course we now know Jimmy's the lifeboat."

Hetty chuckled. "Our plumber friend had a guess too and he came up with Saffron Bun and he calls him Saff whenever he sees him."

Steve sat down and placed the bear on his lap. "Your plumber must be psychic then because this little chap *is* called Saffron Bun."

In the early hours of Monday morning, Simon Berryman suddenly woke, sat up in bed and switched on his lamp. "Jacob Wheatley," he shouted, "his name was Jacob Wheatley."

Sheila half-awake beside him frowned. "Who was Jacob Wheatley?" she yawned.

"The chap who drove the hearse for Dad and the family. It came to me just like that out of the blue. I was thinking about him when I went to bed and that must have caused my brain to get in the right groove. I must ring Hetty and Lottie and tell them."

Sheila glanced at the clock and smiled. "I don't think that's a very good idea. Not at half past five in the morning."

"Damn, I'll never be able to get back to sleep now."

"Anyway, the lodger is no longer a suspect," Sheila reminded him, "and he only ever was because he would have had access to the funeral parlour should it turn out that David was inside Peter's coffin which I'm glad to say, he wasn't."

"True, but I'm sure they'll still be pleased to hear that I've remembered the name at last although I've a sneaky feeling that Jacob died young and drowned while out on the lifeboat. At least I remember someone did but it might not have been him. The poor chap, whoever he was, went overboard during horrendous weather. They tried to get him back on board but the sea dragged him down and there were no more sightings of him until he was washed up on the beach a couple of days later."

"That's dreadful," tutted Sheila, "Poor Jacob or whoever."

"Yes it was dreadful," Simon scowled trying hard to recall the details, "Dad told me about it and it's a bit hazy but it was definitely during the war. It's not easy to remember things that you hear as a child and it's difficult to store them in the old memory, especially if there are no images to go with the facts, if you know what I mean."

Sheila yawned. "Yes, I do."

"Fancy a cup of tea?"

"No thank you." Sheila turned on her side away from the light.

"Oh, well I think I'll have one," Simon climbed out of bed and reached for his dressing gown hanging on the door. "I need to write the name down as well because if I go back to sleep without doing so I'll probably wake later and have forgotten again." He put on his slippers. "Are you sure you don't want a cup of tea?" But Sheila didn't answer. She had gone back to sleep.

"Jacob Wheatley," gasped Hetty, who had answered the phone when Simon rang at nine o'clock. "Well, fancy you remembering. Not that it matters now as he's off the hook."

"Yes, that's what Sheila said."

"Mind you, he still might have been involved. After all he must have known David and so there could have been a rift between them. He did after all live here and so had access to the attic."

Simon laughed. "Yes and lots of other people would have known David too. I'm afraid without a motive or even a body we've nothing to go on and so let's hope he died peacefully in his sleep somewhere up-country when a very old man. He might even still be alive."

Hetty laughed. "I doubt it. If he was born in 1912 he'd be one hundred and five now but I suppose even that's not impossible."

During breakfast, Hetty said that she would like to go to Penzance and make enquiries at any of the art galleries to see if anyone knew anything about S J Choak.

"But why?" Lottie asked, "You know his painting of Old Jimmy has nothing whatsoever to do with David and so forth."

"I know that but I like the picture very much and so want to learn anything I can about the chap that painted it, that's all."

"Fair enough and I'm happy to go with you as I always like a trip to Penzance." She turned to Zac, "What about you, Zac? Do have plans for today?"

"Yep, we're playing volleyball on the beach against some holiday makers who are staying at Sea View Cottage, would you believe?"

"That sounds fun," said Hetty. "I feel quite envious. I used to like volleyball back in my school days but then only because it didn't involve too much running around."

"But that was in the gym," teased Lottie, "I should imagine it's quite hard on the legs when played on sand."

Zac nodded. "It is."

Lottie stood up and dropped two slices of bread in the toaster. "Anyway, we'll leave the key under the plant pot out the back when we go so if you come back for any reason you can get in."

"Okay," Zac finished his breakfast and put his empty plate on the draining board.

"Shall I ask Grace if she'd like to join us?" Hetty asked as Zac left the kitchen.

"Yes, I think you ought as she'll be off home before we know it and we'll miss her when she's gone."

"Yes, we will, she's been like one of the family."

Grace agreed to join them and before they left Hetty took a photograph on her phone of the Old Jimmy painting so that she could show it should anyone have heard of the artist, S J Choak.

At the first gallery they went into there was no-one in authority to answer questions and so they learned nothing at all. However in the second they were very surprised indeed. For the gallery had for one week only an exhibition of West Cornwall's artists and among them were paintings by S J Choak loaned by the members of the public to whom they belonged.

"I don't know what to say," whispered Hetty, as they were approached by a middle aged man in a suit with the name Graham on a badge attached to his lapel.

"Can I help you ladies, at all?"

"Yes, is Mr Choak an accomplished artist?" Grace asked, "I must admit I'm very impressed by his work."

"Was," corrected Graham, "He was an accomplished artist and he died fifty years ago. This exhibition coincides with the half centenary of his death. But his work is recognised all over the country and is greatly sought after by people who like paintings on a nautical theme."

"Yes, I know he's no longer with us because I Googled him the other day," said Hetty, having found her voice, "I have one of his paintings, you see." She took out her phone and showed it to Graham.

"Old Jimmy," he gasped, "you have the painting of Old Jimmy." Graham sat down.

Hetty felt a sudden pang of guilt. "Why are you so surprised?"

"We've been trying to locate it for several years but with no luck."

Hetty felt even more guilty. "I bought it at a car boot sale."

"You bought it at car boot sale." The colour drained from Graham's face.

Hetty nodded. "Yes, for five pounds."

Graham suddenly started to laugh but at the same time he seemed on the verge of tears. "Sorry," he said, "you must think me stupid but I'm in shock."

"Perhaps Hetty's painting is a copy," suggested Lottie, hoping it might make Graham feel better.

Grace nodded. "Yes, perhaps it's a print. Lots of artists have prints made."

Graham shook his head. "There were never any prints made of Choak's work."

"Oh, well you're quite welcome to come and see it to check that it's genuine," said Lottie, "We're only a few miles away in Pentrillick."

"I should like to do that. When would be convenient?"

"We can be there whenever you want," gushed Hetty, "today even because we'll be going back soon."

"I can't make it today because I'm here on my own but if you leave me your phone number I'll give you a ring to arrange a time later in the week."

"Excellent," With enthusiasm Hetty wrote down their address and phone number in her neatest handwriting.

Later that evening Alex called in after work to say his friend had cleaned up the two films found in the suitcase and had offered to bring along the necessary equipment to show them on Tuesday evening.

"How exciting," squealed Hetty, "We'll lay on a bit of food and get in a few bottles of wine. I can't wait to see them."

"I must admit I'm eager to see them as well," acknowledged Alex, "especially if they're taken in and around Pentrillick which I should imagine they are."

"Your friend hasn't said anything about them then?"

Alex shook his head. "No, I told him I wanted them to be as much a surprise to me as they will be to all of you."

Chapter Nineteen

Grace called in for coffee on Tuesday morning and with her she had a bag of chocolate eclairs made by Chloe.

"I see there's a van outside," she said to Hetty who had answered the door, "Is it the carpet fitters?"

"Yes, and we're so excited. Once the carpets are down we'll be ready for the furniture. Not that we're having much because we only need beds, chairs and bedside cabinets. We're so glad Basil suggested built-in wardrobes as they've saved us a lot of space." Hetty closed the door. "Lottie's already made one pair of curtains and of course we'll need some pictures for the plain white walls, but we'll get them from the charity shop. They had quite a lot when we were last in there."

Grace smiled sweetly. "I look forward to seeing it when it's finished and you already have one picture anyway. I'm referring of course to Old Jimmy."

"Oh no, Old Jimmy stays in my room. He's hanging on the wall now opposite the window so that he can look out towards the coast."

"A fitting location for a celebrity lifeboatman and I'm sure he must appreciate it," teased Grace.

"Oh yes, without doubt his smile is broader now than it was when I first brought him home. Having said that we don't actually know that he was a lifeboatman, we just assumed he was because I stupidly claimed that he was our mystery hearse driver who of course we now know was called Jacob Wheatley."

"Good point, I hadn't thought of that but judging by the appearance of Old Jimmy he must either have been a lifeboatman or a fisherman."

"Or perhaps even both."

Hetty led Grace into the kitchen where Lottie was filling a vase with water in order to arrange dahlias which she'd just brought in from the garden.

"I was going to text you but I don't need to now that you've come round," said Hetty, "You see, Alex called in last night to say that the films are ready for us to watch at last and so we've agreed to have a film show this evening. I've already phoned Simon so he'll be here with Sheila and it'd nice if you could join us too."

"Films," Grace looked puzzled, "what films?"

Hetty frowned. "David's films. Surely we've mentioned them to you before?" She took a plate from the cupboard and placed the eclairs on it. "Hmm, they do look nice. I wish I could bake like Chloe."

Grace sat down on a kitchen stool. "Yes, they do, but I've no idea what you're talking about. I mean, what are David's films?"

"Oh dear didn't we tell you? Silly us. Would you like tea or coffee with your éclair?"

"Coffee, please."

"How about you. Lottie?"

"Same for me."

Hetty filled kettle and then spooned coffee granules into three mugs. "We found the films in the suitcase, Grace, along with a cine camera. There were two but of course we had no way of seeing what's on them. Fortunately for us Alex next door has a friend who is into stuff like that and so he took it all away and sorted it out. In retrospect I suppose that's why you hadn't seen or heard of them because Alex had already taken them before we met you."

"But that's amazing. So what are the films of?"

Hetty shrugged her shoulders. "No idea. Probably all fishing stuff, trains and lifeboats, but I hope one of them at least has people on it and hopefully they'll be people whose names have cropped up in our searches. Not that we'll know who they are. I mean, they're hardly likely to be wearing name badges, are they?"

Grace shook her head.

"But we'll be able to recognise David's girlfriend, Edith Triggs," said Lottie, "because Steve had some really nice, clear pictures of her."

"And of course we'll be able to recognise the brothers as well," gushed Hetty, pouring water into the mugs, "because of the photograph that was in the suitcase."

"And Steve Martin had a nice one of him too," Lottie added.

"That's right, he did."

Lottie picked up the vase of flowers to take into the sitting room. "So we'll be able to recognise at least three people providing they're on the films of course. It's a shame Simon's family pictures were damaged because the ones we saw didn't help much at all. Still, never mind. Bring my coffee through please, Het, and the eclairs and let's go into the sitting room where it's nice and sunny."

As Luke Burleigh closed the gate of Fuchsia Cottage early on Tuesday evening, he saw a car pull up further along Blackberry Way outside, he estimated, Primrose Cottage. The slamming of the car doors was followed by the chatter of excited voices, the house door closed and then all fell silent.

The evening felt a little chilly and so Luke zipped up his jacket and as he walked he whistled a happy tune and looked to the sky, mottled with shades of orange and pink in the west. And then he stopped in his tracks remembering he had put on a clean pair of jeans and had forgotten to transfer his wallet from his other pair. Tutting, he retraced his steps and returned indoors where Natalie was watching television. After explaining the reason for his sudden return home he again left the house and resumed his walk to the pub.

As he neared Primrose Cottage something caused him to slow his pace. A dark figure was crouching outside the front garden wall of the house. In its hand the figure held a large container and its behaviour was furtive and suspicious.

Luke's pace slowed to a halt when the figure sprang forwards and dashed through the open gates. To make sure he was not seen, Luke stepped from the road and onto the grass verge in front of the boundary wall of Hillside and, from behind the cover of a fuchsia bush, he listened and watched for any further activity. The figure whoever it was had not gone inside the house or even knocked on the door. For the door had not opened and no cheerful voices had welcomed the mystery person to cross the threshold. Luke crouched down low. From within the house he could hear lively chatter and joyful laughter, yet outside all was quiet. Intuitively he kept still. Something was wrong and he was determined to remain in his hiding place until the dark figure reappeared or the reason for his unease became apparent.

Inside Primrose Cottage, Hetty and Lottie offered glasses of wine to their guests: neighbours, Tommy and Kitty and Alex and Ginny; friends: Bernie the Boatman and his wife, Veronica, Sid the plumber and of course Simon and Sheila Berryman.

Ginny pulled the curtains to darken the room and while Alex set up a projector ready for the film show, as instructed by his friend, Zac and Emma were busy in the kitchen putting snacks into dishes for the guests.

"What was that?" Zac suddenly asked, glancing around the kitchen.

"What was what?"

"I don't know. It was a sort of clicking noise."

Emma shrugged her shoulders. "I don't know. I didn't hear anything but I'm sure it's nothing to worry about."

Zac reached up to a shelf where a radio sat, turned down the volume and listened for any more sounds. He tutted. "I must have dreamt it."

"Yes, come on, let's take these in the other room because we don't want to miss anything."

From behind the fuchsia bush, Luke heard footsteps walking across the tarmacked driveway and then they stopped. Someone coughed and he heard what sounded like liquid sloshing around in a vessel. The sound of splashing followed and then he heard the shuffling of feet and more splashing. Luke lifted his head. His nose twitched. Petrol. He could smell petrol. He scrambled to his feet and dashed forward just in time to see someone wearing a hooded top push lighted paper through the letterbox and then throw a match onto the clump of pampas grass swaying in front of the sitting room window. As Luke ran forwards shouting and waving his fists, the feathery plumes of the pampas grass burst into flames and the figure ran away.

Inside Primrose Cottage, Hetty frowned. "Who's that outside shouting?"

No-one answered but Zac nearest the sitting room door, jumped to his feet and switched on the light. "I can smell smoke and hear crackling." He opened the door and looked into the hallway. The doormat and the hall table were on fire and flames were rapidly spreading across the floor. As everyone followed Zac into the hallway, Alex dialled 999 on his mobile phone and asked for the police and fire brigade. Tommy meanwhile suggested they all make their way into the kitchen to get out of the back door, but when they got there, the door was locked.

"Where's the key?" Tommy shouted, his hands in the air.

"It should be in the lock," screamed Hetty, in panic, "we never take it out."

"Well it's not there now." Tommy looked on the floor and lifted up the doormat.

Emma's eye's filled with tears. Zac squeezed her hand.

"The clicking sound," whispered Emma, biting her bottom lip, "the clicking sound you heard must have been someone locking the door."

"The dining room or living room windows," shouted Lottie, leading the way, "We can get out of one of them."

"Not the dining room," groaned Tommy, "the door's blocked because the carpet's on fire."

They all rushed into the living room where Lottie yanked back the curtains. Everyone screamed when they saw the pampas grass outside the window was engulfed in flames.

Luke, torn between chasing the arsonist and helping the victims of the fire chose the latter and frantically ran around outside the house looking for water. He jumped when Grace carrying a bottle of wine suddenly appeared through the gate.

"What the hell's going on?" She screamed. "What are you doing here? What have you done?"

"Done," shouted Luke, "I've not done anything apart from trying to find water to put the damn fire out. There are people trapped in there. Listen, you can hear them screaming."

Grace threw the bottle of wine into a lavender bush and rushed forwards. "There's a tap down the side of the house. Come with me, I'll show you."

Luke followed Grace to the tap. He shouted with relief when he saw it had a hose attached. Without wasting another second he turned the tap on full and ran to the front of the house. With a mighty kick he knocked the door open and doused the flames with water.

Trembling, Grace stood by his side biting her nails and praying that the fire would be extinguished. When she heard the sound of sirens ringing through the night air she fell to her knees and wept.

Chapter Twenty

The following morning as Lottie and Hetty washed down the kitchen walls, blackened by the fire, both expressed their thanks that the house was not at all badly harmed as only the hallway was in need of repair work. Basil had already been round to survey the damage and they were grateful, for it had occurred to them after the fire brigade and police had departed that they had forgotten to take out a policy for house insurance. Apart from the hallway, the rest of the house was just blackened here and there; something the sisters agreed would respond well to some elbow grease and a coat or two of paint. The smell of smoke was also prevalent in every room and so they opened all of the windows throughout the house including the new rooms in the attic and thanked God that the sun was shining and there were no grey clouds looming.

To their amazement just before lunchtime a team of volunteers arrived from the village to help clean the walls, along with neighbours, Tommy and Kitty and Chloe from Tuzzy-Muzzy, who had just finished the guests' rooms.

"No Grace?" said Hetty, as Chloe pulled on a pair of rubber gloves.

Chloe shook her head. "No, poor thing, she looked really pale during breakfast and said she was going to lie down for a while so not to bother with her room today. She thinks she might have inhaled too much smoke."

Hetty scowled. "Really, but she arrived late and I never set foot in the house."

"I expect if the truth be known she's still in shock," said Lottie, sympathetically, "It must have been dreadful for her seeing the flames and realising we were all trapped inside."

Chloe looked at the remains of the burnt-out door. "Have you got anyone to fix that yet? I mean you can't live here with no door."

Hetty smiled. "Yes, it's all in hand. In fact Basil's out getting us one right now and he's promised it'll be done by the end of the day."

"And he's going to re-plaster the hallway next week," Lottie added, "and for that we're extremely grateful."

Meanwhile, the police were confident that there would be CCTV footage on one of the petrol stations in West Cornwall showing someone filling a petrol can in recent days. And as Vince's garage was the nearest to the scene of the crime, they made his business their first call. Vince, already familiar with the malicious acts against the sisters - the brakes in particular - was more than willing to oblige and provided the footage requested. To the delight of the two officers sent out to investigate, they hit the jackpot first time. For the previous afternoon someone had driven onto the garage forecourt and filled up a red five litre petrol can identical to the empty one they had found discarded over the garden wall of Tuzzy-Muzzy along with a black hooded top, size 14 which still bore the price tag. The person in question was a dark haired female and the police instantly recognised her as someone who had been present at Primrose Cottage on the night of the fire. Furthermore, she was someone who they believed to be a friend of the two ladies who lived in said house.

Inside her room, Grace hastily pulled out her suitcase from the gap beside her dressing table and the wall. All she could think was that she must pack and leave Cornwall as quickly as possible. Things had got out of hand and she needed to make a hasty exit before the police put two and two together and made four. Hurriedly she grabbed every item of clothing which hung in the wardrobe and tossed them into a heap on the bed. She then knelt down on the floor but before she even had time to unzip the suitcase, she heard a knock on the door. With fingers crossed hoping that it was just Chloe knocking to see if she was feeling better, she cautiously went to the door. Chloe's husband, Colin was standing on the landing and with him were two uniformed police officers.

Inside the police station, Grace sat with her clasped hands resting on her lap. Her face was pale and her eyes red from crying. After intense questioning she had finally admitted to starting the fire at Primrose Cottage but she refused to say why she had done so. In fact apart from confessing to the arson attack she refused to say anything at all.

When Hetty and Lottie heard the news they were devastated. Both sat in a daze as they tried to make sense of Grace's actions. Even the thought of a cup of tea was, they considered, not a helpful remedy for their distress.

It was the police who had told them of Grace's arrest. They had called just before five o'clock when the last of the volunteers had returned home for the day and Basil was in the throes of handing over the keys to the newly fitted door. Zac was already out having gone to join his friends who were having a barbecue on the beach.

"Strange, isn't it," whispered Hetty, when she finally found her voice, "that someone we thought to be a friend has turned out to be a foe and the person we thought to be a foe has turned has out to be a friend? I'm obviously referring to Luke."

"Yes, Luke has turned out to be our saviour. As for Grace, I can't for the life of me see why she did it," Lottie croaked.

"Me neither and if she's saying nothing then we'll probably never know for sure. Having said that, it must be something to do with the suitcase but as far as I can see there is nothing at all to connect Grace to the Berrymans or the Tregears and as yet we have no concrete reason to believe that anything untoward happened to David anyway. It's all most peculiar."

Feeling in need of company other than that of each other, Hetty and Lottie walked down to the Crown and Anchor in the evening hoping the atmosphere there might lift their spirits. As they sat down with their drinks, the first person they saw was Luke Burleigh playing darts with Vince Royale from the garage.

Hetty gulped. "Oh dear. I think it's time to eat humble pie," she said, rising from her seat, "I didn't get the chance to say anything last night with all the flashing lights and pandemonium and I really do need to clear my conscience."

Lottie rose also. "Me too and so I shall go with you."

"I suppose the Grace thing means you won't want to have a pond warming party on my last night now." Zac looked a little downcast as he sat in the kitchen the following morning with a mug of coffee. "I can't say as I blame you. I liked Grace even though she must be bonkers."

"Oh Zac, of course we'll have the party," said Lottie, patting his shoulder affectionately, "Don't you agree, Het?"

"Absolutely, because when all's said and done nothing has really changed. I mean we know Grace started the fire but there's no way she did the other things, especially the brakes because she was with us in the car when they failed."

Zac looked puzzled. "But why did she start the fire? I was talking about it last night with my friends and we all agreed it was a weird thing to do unless she's a compulsive arsonist and none of us knew that. I mean it's hardly something she would tell you about, is it? If she was, I mean."

Lottie actually laughed. "I know it's not funny but imaging someone as lady-like as Grace being a compulsive arsonist conjures up a comical image."

"Yes, it does," sighed Hetty, "Perhaps looking after her aged mother had a strange effect on her for some reason."

"No, I can't believe that," said Lottie, "and even if it had, the lady has gone now and with her passing any stress Grace might have encountered should have gone too."

"Well, whatever it is or was, the pampas grass is no more," chuckled Hetty, "and I'm grateful for that."

"Yes, but I daresay before long it'll send up new shoots and end up even bigger and healthier than before."

"Humph, it won't" grunted Hetty, "because after poor Peter Tregear's funeral tomorrow, God rest his soul, I shall be digging it out once and for all."

Lottie chuckled as she stood up to put the kettle on. "And I think I shall give you a helping hand."

In the afternoon the new furniture arrived for the attic bedrooms and so Hetty and Zac assembled the beds, one double and two singles, while Lottie hung the curtains she had made and cleaned the windows also. When everything was in place, they made up the beds and then all walked down to the village where Hetty and Lottie went to the charity shop to look at pictures and Zac went to the Crown and Anchor to meet Kyle and Emma.

No customers were in the charity shop when they arrived but Maisie and Daisy were on duty. They both apologised for not helping with washing down the paintwork but said they couldn't get away as they were both working in the shop. Nevertheless, they were keen to hear the latest news about the fire and to hear if there were any more developments regarding David Tregear. Hetty and Lottie willingly brought them up to date and said there were still many questions that needed answers.

"One thing you might be able to help us with though is Jacob Wheatley," said Hetty, "Does the name mean anything to you? I keep meaning to ask Kitty but so far haven't remembered as my poor old brain is cluttered up with names and dates."

"You might never have heard of him though because Simon thinks he might have drowned during the war while out on the lifeboat," added Lottie.

"Old Jacob, no he didn't drown," smiled Daisy, "at least the Jacob we knew didn't but he was on the lifeboat, wasn't he, Maisie?"

Maisie nodded her head. "Yes, he was because he used to tell us about it when we were kids, didn't he?"

"Yes, the lifeboat house had closed down by then of course. He worked up at Grange Farm as well and he lived to be a ripe old age. In fact I think he was ninety two when he died. He outlived Emily that I do know. Emily was his wife and they lived in one of houses along the main road here."

"Why do you want to know?" Maisie asked.

"No reason really," Lottie was determined not to let on they had suspected him of murdering David and hiding his body in Peter's coffin. "It's just his name cropped up because he lodged at Primrose Cottage during the war."

"Did he really? A bit before our time." Maisie looked thoughtful. "He and Emily had a couple of children but I can't remember their names. Neither of them are in the area anyway now."

"They were Stephen and Rebecca," said Daisy and they'd be around eighty years old by now."

Maisie groaned. "I suppose they would. How time flies."

When several customers came in Hetty and Lottie went to look at the pictures. They found four they liked, paid for them, took them home and hung them on the walls.

"Finished at last," said Lottie, "and I'm as pleased as punch."

Hetty smiled broadly. "Yes, me too."

Chapter Twenty-One

Sid Moore, having finished an arduous plumbing job in Penzance the previous day decided to take a day off work, relax and do a bit of gardening. With spade in hand he went to his vegetable plot to dig over the area where broad beans had been, in order to put in a row each of lettuce and spring onions. As he dug he was thinking: his thoughts dominated by the peculiar case of David Tregear.

"I dunno," he said to a robin perched on a nearby branch, "whatever can have happened to the lad? Did he do a runner as rumour suggested or did he meet a more sinister end? And as for Grace Dunkerley I'm completely miffed as to why such a friendly and likable lady as she would do something as daft and evil as to try and set light to Hetty and Lottie's place."

As he pushed his spade into the rich brown earth he was conscious of a few people gathered in the churchyard opposite where the remains of Peter Tregear were to be re-buried. He sighed. "And as for poor Peter, it's such a shame the lad were disturbed from his sleeping after all these years for no good reason but hopefully he'll be able to rest in peace now."

The robin watched as Sid continued to dig. When his spade hit something solid, he scraped earth to one side and then pulled out a stone. Beside it was a wishbone no doubt from a chicken or a turkey which had long since been part of someone's dinner. "A distant cousin of yours no doubt," he chuckled to the robin who had flown down to peck over the crumbly rich soil. Sid tossed both stone and bone to one side;

as they hit the ground, a crystal clear vision flashed through his mind.

"Oh my God," he shouted, as an icy shiver ran down his spine, "Oh my God, why didn't I think of it before?" And with spade in hand, he ran from his garden, crossed the road and climbed over the wall into the oldest part of the churchyard. He then ran, jumping over graves, flower vases and small shrubs towards the area where the funeral party were gathered beside the grave of Peter Tregear.

"Stop," he shouted, waving his spade. "Stop, don't bury the lad. At least not for a minute or two."

The small gathering stared at the plumber who was trying hard to catch his breath.

"Are you okay, Sid?" Alex asked.

Sid nodded. "Yes," he panted, "it's just that." He looked at Vicar Sam. "Forgive me, Sam, reverend, vicar, sir." He then leaned forward, pulled out the green fabric lining the grave and jumped six feet down.

Hetty and Lottie gasped; both felt light headed and linked arms to support each other. Vicar Sam dropped his prayer book, the pallbearers lowered Peter's coffin down onto the grass, Tommy's jaw dropped, and Kitty quickly sat down on Peter's upturned headstone before her legs gave way. No-one in the small group spoke but gradually they all moved closer and peered into the deep hole where Sid gently dug into the compacted earth with his spade. Slowly a mound of loosened soil piled up around his feet. Hetty gulped when she and everyone else gathered realised the reason behind Sid's extraordinary behaviour and no-one was surprised when Sid put aside the spade, knelt and gently pushed away the loosened earth with his hands. For he had struck something solid and as he scraped away the earth it was clear for all to see that that something was a skull.

Sid scrambled to his feet and looked up to the faces peering down at him and Vicar Sam offered his hands to pull Sid back up to the surface.

"I think," muttered Alex, as Sid clambered onto the grass, "that the mystery of David Tregear is part-solved at last."

Chapter Twenty-Two

In the early evening, Hetty and Lottie along with Zac and Emma left Primrose Cottage for the short walk to their neighbours, Alex and Ginny's house. As Hetty locked the front door a look of satisfaction crossed her face as she glanced at the spot where the pampas grass was no more. The scorched clump had not been easy to remove: in fact it had taken the sisters considerably longer than they had anticipated but they considered their exertion worthwhile and looked forward to buying something they both liked to fill the gaping void.

It was the same group of people that had gathered a few nights before that sat together at Hillside with glasses of wine eagerly waiting to see the films found in the attic. The change of venue from Primrose Cottage to Hillside was because Hetty and Lottie felt their home wasn't welcoming with its scorched hallway, cracked plaster and the persistent smell of smoke.

The films were in black and white; the first began with two young men: the same two as on the old photograph in the suitcase. They were on a beach instantly recognisable as Pentrillick. One of the young men, they knew to be David, was painting his boat Goliath, and the other, Peter, was sitting on the sand carving a small piece of wood. The camera then must have been handed to David for now a woman was on the beach. An older woman who they assumed to be, Florence, their mother. She was sitting on the sand beside Peter, laughing self-consciously.

"The camera must have belonged to David," reasoned Hetty, "since he seems to be in control which of course would explain why it was in his suitcase."

"Yes, it was no doubt a hobby of his because cinematography was very popular back then but it was also very expensive," remarked Alex. "An expensive hobby for a humble train driver."

"Well, I daresay he was helped out financially by his mother," said Ginny, "after all she did own the hotel."

"And maybe his stepfather too," added Simon, "because between them, Harold and Florence owned the two most profitable businesses in Pentrillick."

Emma pointed at the screen. "I wonder if this film is actually showing the chap who we assume to be Peter carving the model of his brother's boat, Goliath."

"Well spotted. Yes, it looks like it could be," agreed Simon, "and that's probably why he's sitting near to it on the beach."

Hetty shuddered, thinking of the earlier discovery in the churchyard. "I've gone all goosepimply. Seeing the brothers alive and well, I mean. This morning's aborted funeral was quite shocking but I'm glad we've found David at last."

Lottie sighed deeply. "Yes, when this film was made little did they know what lay before them."

"Oh, looks like that's the end of the first film," Alex stood up as it abruptly finished. "You might find the next one is more interesting because apparently there are other people on it and it's quite a bit longer."

"You've had a sneak preview then," teased Hetty, as Alex changed the films over. "You told me you didn't want to know what was on them."

"No, I've not had a sneak preview because I meant it when I said I wanted to see them for the first time along with all of you. It was Paul, my film enthusiast friend, who said about there being more people on the reel he's marked as two which as I say, is also a little longer."

"More wine?" Ginny asked, as she walked around topping up glasses, "and please help yourself to nibbles. And there are also more cans of lager in the fridge for the non-wine drinkers amongst you."

Zac went into the kitchen to fetch cans for himself, Sid and Emma. And because no-one was driving, everyone else had wine, for Ginny had insisted Simon and Sheila must stay at Hillside for the night rather than drive all the way back to Truro.

"Well, as lovely as the first film was it hasn't in any way helped us find out who killed poor David, has it?" sighed Hetty.

"But you don't need to worry about it anymore," laughed Ginny, as she sat down on a stool, "it's up to the police to figure it out now. You've done your bit by being so adamant that something horrid had happened to him."

"Yes, I suppose you're right," conceded Hetty, "but I don't like to leave a job half done."

"Are you ready to see the second film now?" Alex asked.

The answer was yes from everyone.

"Right, here goes." Alex started the film and then sat down.

"Surely this one's taken in the grounds of the Pentrillick Hotel," said Kitty, as the film flickered on the screen, "because that building in the background is definitely the hotel. I recognise the fancy balustrades around the terrace."

"Most likely," Lottie agreed, "because the Tregear family would have owned it when the film was taken. I don't recognise it though but then I've never seen the hotel from the back."

All eyes were glued to the screen when the camera turned towards a young couple sitting on a lawn arms round each other laughing. With them were Peter, lying on his stomach reading a book and an older couple drinking from china teacups.

Simon gasped and leaned forwards in his chair. "Good grief, that's my mum and dad," he whispered, pointing to the younger couple, "but if these films were taken before 1942 then it would have been before they were married. Now it's my turn to have gone all goosepimply."

"Oh, but that's lovely," cried Lottie, "I should dearly love to have a little film of my parents when they were young," she looked at Hetty, "or should I say our parents."

Hetty nodded. "Yes and I agree. Photographs are good but film captures so much more and this particular film is excellent quality considering its age."

"Yes," agreed Alex, "Paul has done a splendid job of cleaning them up."

Hetty sighed. "Such a shame there's no sound as I'd love to hear what they're saying and know what their voices sounded like too."

Lottie nodded. "Same here."

"So, who are the older couple?" Sheila asked, "I can see that the lady is Florence - David and Peter's mother, but who is the older man?"

Simon smiled. "He's Harold Berryman, my grandfather and Florence's second husband. He's much younger there than I remember him of course but I'd recognise that smile anywhere."

Suddenly the camera turned to a young woman with blonde hair sitting on some steps with Saffron Bun on her lap. From one hand she was blowing kisses to the cameraman; the other hand held Saffron Bun's waving arm."

"And that's Edith Triggs," shrieked Lottie, "Steve Martin's grandmother who was of course, David's girlfriend."

"Hence the kisses," giggled Emma.

"And she's the one who called a spade a spade," chuckled Hetty. "She doesn't look like she'd say boo to a goose."

Ginny nodded. "But looks can be deceiving."

"Edith Triggs," gasped Alex, "Oh dear, and it's just occurred to me that we ought to have asked young Steve to join us tonight."

"Don't worry, we did ask him," Hetty divulged, "but he said regrettably he couldn't make it because it's his girlfriend's birthday today and so they're going out."

"Oh well done and perhaps we can show him the film some other time."

Lottie nodded. "Yes, I'm sure he'd love to see it and even have a copy if possible."

"And if it is, I'd like a copy as well," said Simon.

"Well, we're not learning a great deal, are we?" laughed Ginny, "but it's very entertaining."

"It is," agreed Lottie, "I love glimpsing back to bygone days."

The camera then turned away from Edith on the steps to a young woman walking across the lawn waving both arms.

"Ah, so who's this?" Hetty asked.

"A shapely brunette," grinned Sid, "with an unfortunate limp."

Simon gasped. "That's Polly, Aunt Polly. I remember now. She did have a limp because she'd had polio when she was a child."

"Hmm, sadly it was very common back then," sighed Hetty.

"Yes, and that," declared Lottie, "would be why she avoided conscription, Het."

Hetty slapped herself on the knee. "Yes, of course. Well done, Lottie."

As Polly neared the camera, Lottie's hands flew up to her mouth. "Oh my goodness, oh my goodness. Look at the bodice of her dress, Het."

Hetty gasped and put down her wine glass as her eyes were drawn to Polly's dress. Pinned to the yoke was a brooch…a beautiful dragonfly brooch… identical to the one frequently worn by Grace."

Chapter Twenty-Three

When Grace entered the interview room in the police station, she knew by the look on Detective Inspector Fox's face that the game was up. She sat down when asked so to do.

"You know, don't you?" She sighed. "They've watched the films, haven't they?" She hung her head and her lips quivered. "I didn't know whether or not she'd be on them but thought the chances were that she would and that Simon would recognise her or worse still that she'd be wearing the brooch. She always wore it you see. It was her pride and joy."

Detective Inspector Fox leaned back in his chair and joined his hands together. "Care to tell me about it, Ms Dunkerley?"

Grace nodded. "Yes, I might as well now. There's nothing to be gained by keeping quiet and if the truth be known, I feel I owe it to Hetty and Lottie. I've treated them shamefully and for that I am truly sorry."

The inspector nodded. "When you're ready, in your own time."

"I don't know where to start."

"Perhaps you could start by telling me of your relationship to Polly Berryman. I assume she is the lady to whom you referred as she."

Grace nodded. "Yes, and she's my mother. At least she was until she died earlier this year."

"So I suggest you start at the beginning."

Grace took in a deep breath. "Before I start, I must emphasise that the names of my parents as told to Hetty and Lottie are not true. At least, my mother's name was incorrect. I said her name was Anne Smith, you see. Silly really, but for some reason it was the first name that came into my head. Stupidly, I wrote it down when no-one was looking on the back of a Bernie the Boatman business card which I'd picked up in the post office and kept in my bag. Not that I was planning to go fishing. I just thought it would be nice to keep. You know, as a memento. I wrote Anne Smith down because I didn't want to forget the name in case it cropped up again and then it must have fallen from my bag when I was in the pub buying a round of drinks." The memory caused Grace to smile. "You've probably guessed who found it. Thank goodness I'd not opted for an unusual name." Grace noticed the inspector was frowning. "I'm sorry. I've gone off at a tangent, haven't I? I'll try and stick to the facts from now on."

"I'd appreciate that," said the inspector, "So, can I take it that your father was a Dunkerley?"

"Yes, he was Reg Dunkerley and you'll never meet a kinder or more generous man than he was." She sighed. "Anyway, we're not here to discuss the virtues of my father, are we, so I suppose I must get back to the salient facts."

Detective Inspector Fox nodded. "Yes, if you please."

"Right, well, my mother's name was Polly and for most of my life I knew very little about her family. I didn't even know that she came from Cornwall. In fact I knew nothing at all except that my mother's maiden name was Berryman and that her mother, my grandmother was called Ethel and apparently I looked very much like her. My grandmother died young giving birth to my mother, and all Mum had to remember her by was this brooch which apparently she and my grandmother both treasured." Grace touched the dragonfly attached to the lapel of her jacket with affection. "And now the brooch that Mother so loved has proved to be her undoing. Silly really, but it never occurred to me that wearing it would be my downfall too." Grace laughed. "I was even stupid enough to tell Hetty and

Lottie that it had belonged to my grandmother and then my mother and now me. When they admired it, why couldn't I have said that I'd bought it in a flea market or something like that? Sometimes I question my own stupidity."

"It's usually the little things that result in people getting caught," said the inspector, "and I speak from years of experience."

Grace nodded. "Yes, I can see the logic there. Anyway, there's nothing much more I can say about the Berrymans. On the other hand I know a lot about my father's family. They lived in Derbyshire. Dad was a foreman in a factory where Mum worked and after they were married they settled in a cottage only a couple of miles away from where Granny and Gramps Dunkerley lived. Dad, who as I've already told you was called Reg, died when he was sixty two and Mum lived until she was ninety eight. Amazing really considering she'd had polio when she was a child." Her voice softened. "She died earlier this year just after Easter. It was April the twentieth and the blackest day of my life." Grace paused and looked to the window where a nearby building blocked out the sunlight and cast a dark shadow over the street below. She then returned her focus to the inspector. "On her deathbed, my mother said that she wanted to unburden herself from something which had troubled her much of late. I expected it to be something trivial: petty theft perhaps or a small matter of deceit."

"But you found it was something much more sinister." The inspector almost looked sympathetic.

"Yes. You see, it was my mother who took the life of David Tregear for no other reason than that she wanted to own and run the Pentrillick Hotel. She ran the bar there, you see, and became addicted to gin and, I'm ashamed to say, was often drunk, although she told me that she hid it well. At least she thought she did. We'll never know for sure, will we? Anyway, thankfully, I never saw her drunk. Apparently she gave it all up long before I was born and became tee-total. As a teenager I was miffed as to why she was so anti-drink. I knew it wasn't for religious reasons because she was an atheist. Anyway, to get back to the story, she told me that on the day that David died she'd been drinking and had then gone to Primrose Cottage to see her brother George. He was not in and so she let herself into the house using the key she knew was hidden underneath the doormat. While she was there David called. To say Mother and David had never got on well would be an understatement. And because Mother was infatuated with Peter, she told David that she wished he'd died instead of his brother. In retaliation he called her a drunken gold-digger and said she'd only been interested in Peter because she wanted to get her hands on the hotel and drink, drink, drink. She was furious because he'd hit the nail on the head and so her response was to scream, shout and verbally abuse him. She wanted her words to hurt him just as his words had hurt her. But to her annoyance, he just laughed and the more she screamed at him the more he laughed. Mother was livid. She hated being laughed at and in a rage she killed him, but she wouldn't tell me how. I wrote down what she told me so that I'd be able to remember. Now I wish I hadn't because her words are firmly ensconced in my brain and torture me daily. As I've said, I don't know how Mother killed him but just that she did."

"According to the pathology report there is evidence of a stab wound to the chest and that was most likely the cause of death."

What little colour there was drained from Grace's face. "She stabbed him! Oh no. How could she?"

The inspector nodded. "It looks that way. Yes."

Grace looked at the floor to hide her tears. The inspector handed her a tissue. "When you're ready, please continue," he asked.

Grace nodded. "Of course." She wiped her eyes and sat up straight. "When it hit my mother that David was dead she panicked. She needed help to dispose of the body and so she asked her brother George what she should do. She told me that George was furious with her; frightened too, but he had to help to safeguard the family name. He greatly admired his father, you see, and the Berrymans were after all well respected undertakers. As it happened the nature of the family business was opportune as it meant they had the means of burying David where he'd never ever be found. Peter's grave was dug by the sexton and once done, George and my mother went out in the dead of night and dug deeper still until they had enough room for David. After putting him in the bottom of the grave, they covered him with earth, tampered it down with their feet so that no-one would be any the wiser. The excess earth they put into sacks and scattered it in George's garden at Primrose Cottage. The plan worked. Peter was buried the next day and everyone was oblivious of the fact that he was not alone in his grave. Mother said she was relieved the plan had worked but the guilt made George ill and for a while he was off work sick."

The inspector poured himself a tumbler of water from the jug on the table and topped up Grace's tumbler too. "Out of curiosity. Did your mother tell you where the body was hidden between the time of death and its burial?"

"Yes, yes, she did. It was in the garage wrapped in an old blanket. Fortunately for mother and George, Jacob Wheatley, George's lodger, was away for a couple of nights visiting relatives somewhere or other and wasn't due back until the day of the funeral."

"I see. Please continue."

"Florence, who was Peter and David's mother, was already worried because David had not been seen for several days and so after Peter's funeral she asked my mother to help her look through his room at the hotel to see if they could find any indication as to where he might have gone. Mother, of course, obliged and to the distress of poor Florence they found David's personal things were missing. You know, shaving stuff, identity card and so forth. His suitcase was gone too and a carving of his boat done by his brother Peter which he treasured. Of course, Mother already knew the missing items were gone because she and George had removed them the day after David died. Or should I say, the day after Mother killed him. I still can't believe she did it, but Mother told Florence that it looked as though David had run away, probably because he was afraid of being 'called up' like his brother. Florence conceded that it was the only plausible explanation and eventually accepted that she might not see him again before the end of the war. But of course he never came home."

Detective Inspector Fox looked puzzled. "Okay, so if your mother wanted the hotel so badly why did she leave Cornwall?"

"Quite simply because George's wife, Betty, who was of course Simon's mother, got wind of what her husband and sister-in-law had done and so my mother, again while drunk, pushed her down the stairs and made it look like an accident. Mother assured me that George never knew what she'd done but he was heartbroken after losing his wife and for that reason she left the area because she couldn't bear to see him so upset over something for which she was responsible, not once but twice. In fact it was the guilt of hurting her brother so badly that brought my mother to her senses. She stopped drinking, met my father, had me and blocked out the horrors of the past from her memory."

"Until she was on her deathbed."

"Yes, until she was on her deathbed."

"So what was it that your mother told you that made you come to Cornwall?"

Grace took in a deep breath. "The suitcase, the damn suitcase. You see, she told me that the possessions she and George had taken from David's room at the hotel were hidden beneath floorboards in the attic of somewhere called Primrose Cottage in a Cornish village called Pentrillick where the family had all lived. Apparently George paid Peter to board out the loft after he bought the house just before the war broke out in 1939." Grace paused to take a sip of water.

"Having the attic boarded out it seems was very opportune," said the inspector, "as not many are even today."

"Very true and I suppose when George put the case there he hoped that it would never be found." Grace half-smiled. "I must confess that I took a lot of what my mother told me with a pinch of salt. I mean, she was ninety eight years old but even at that age she read a lot of novels and murder mysteries were her favourite genre. It occurred to me that she might have muddled fact with fiction and the suitcase didn't exist."

"But you had to make sure?"

"Yes. I Googled Pentrillick and found that Primrose Cottage was next to a guest house and so it seemed the obvious place to come and stay. Imagine my horror when I met Hetty and Lottie and discovered that the suitcase not only existed but that it had actually been found."

"And so you offered to help find out something of David Tregear's past already knowing exactly what had happened to him?"

"Yes, and I was relieved to realise there was nothing in the suitcase to link him to me. No photograph of, or mention of my mother and so even though I thought it likely that her name would eventually crop up in searches I knew she would be difficult to trace because no-one would have any idea where she had gone and whom she had married if indeed married she had. There was no evidence to suggest that at all."

"But you knew nothing of the films?"

Grace shook her head. "No, they had already been taken away by Alex and so all I saw were David's personal things like clothing, the boat, the teddy bear and so forth."

"So why did you feel it necessary to poison Simon Berryman?"

"Hetty told me that he had a few old photos of the family and I thought my mother might be on one of them wearing the brooch. It was never my intention to kill him. I just wanted to make him ill for a while during which time I hoped he'd forget about the pictures and not visit Pentrillick again."

"And the phone calls and the letter bomb?"

"The phone calls were done simply to scare Hetty and Lottie but when I saw they were having no effect I made up the letter bomb for the same reason." She laughed, "But it seemed nothing I did in any way budged the sisters from their mission. They were very persistent and I admire them for that."

Detective Inspector Fox leaned back in his chair. "And yet you tampered with the brakes on the sisters' car. Surely that wasn't done simply to frighten them."

"It was, honestly, I just wanted to scare them. You know, make them think there was some nutcase out there who wanted them dead. My logic was that Hetty would be the driver when next they took the car out. She's been driving for years, you see and so I reckoned she'd automatically pull on the hand brake when the foot pedal was ineffectual. The problem was, when they next went out, Lottie drove and she had only passed her test quite recently. And to make matters worse, Hetty was seated in the back, her movement restricted by her seatbelt. But she freed herself eventually and pulled on the handbrake. I can't believe that I didn't do it myself but I was terrified and couldn't think straight. Everything appeared to go in slow motion and so my reactions were pitifully slow too."

"So why were you in the car when you knew the brakes were not working?"

"I had no choice. I went round to see Hetty and Lottie and they said they were going to Pentrillick House to see David Tregear's boat. They asked me to go with them. I couldn't think of a good enough reason not to go and so had to say yes. Serves me right, I suppose."

"So where did you learn about car mechanics?"

Grace smiled. "My father. He said that in order for anyone to be a good driver they needed to have some knowledge of how the engine worked. And so after my first driving lesson when I was seventeen he lifted the bonnet of his car, pointed out the different parts of the engine and told me their purpose. And although much has changed since those days, I'm talking of 1975, I've always kept up with how things work."

"Tell me about the fire?"

Grace's shoulders slumped. "The fire was a moment of madness. When I heard about the films and how they intended to watch them that night, I didn't know what to do. I panicked. I couldn't think clearly at first. And then I thought of starting a fire. I bought a petrol can and filled it at the garage. It was never my intention to harm anyone. I just wanted the damn films destroyed."

"You were prepared to risk all those lives just to destroy the films?"

"No, because I knew they'd get out alive. I mean, most people die in fires when they happen at night and they're sleeping. I wasn't concerned too much about damage to the property because the insurance would cover the cost of repairs and I knew Hetty disliked the pampas grass so in a way I thought I was doing her a favour."

"You didn't know then that they had no insurance?"

"What! Oh no, didn't they? Oh, that's terrible." Grace's voice croaked with emotion.

"Apparently not."

"I'm so sorry."

"Before you started the fire did you lock the back door?"

"Yes," Grace hung her head, "When Hetty said about the film show I crept into the kitchen and removed the key so that I could lock it later from the outside."

The inspector shook his head slowly. "They could all have died."

"No, no, because I knew they'd get out somehow. I had to make it a little difficult though in order to ensure the films were destroyed. Anyway, part of my plan once I'd discarded the petrol can and the top I'd worn which I'd bought that afternoon, was to arrive in time to put out the fire and save the day but Luke Burleigh got there first which was probably just as well because when I heard the screaming I became a trembling wreck."

The inspector leaned back and folded his arms. "And you did all of this to prevent skeletons tumbling from your closet. A little extreme, don't you think just to protect your name?"

Grace shook her head. "But I didn't do it to protect *my* name. I did it to protect my partner of these past twenty years. My darling John, he's a barrister, you see and I didn't want this to tarnish his spotless reputation." She bowed her head. "But I have failed him dismally."

Chapter Twenty-Four

"I'm glad," whispered Hetty, when Alex called round on Sunday morning to say that Grace had been released on bail, "but I'm not sure that I want to see her again. I mean, I can understand her feeling the way that she did but she could have killed us both and Simon too."

"I think if that's what she'd wanted to do then she would have done so," reasoned Alex, "after all, the police said although Simon was poisoned the amount of poison administered was not sufficient to kill anyone but just to make them ill."

"But what about the brakes incident? Surely it was only luck or providence that saved us that day," cried Hetty.

"True, but she probably thought you'd use the handbrake," said Alex.

Lottie nodded. "Which you did, Het. And had you been driving instead of me we'd have stopped before we reached the bottom of Long Lane."

"Well, whatever: it's very sad though because I really liked Grace and I feel betrayed. I feel cross." Hetty sighed deeply.

"That's quite understandable," sympathised Alex, "Anyway, I must go and I'll see you both later."

"Yes, of course, I'll see you out," Hetty walked with him to the door. As she returned to the kitchen, Lottie looked towards the ceiling having heard footsteps in the bathroom above. "Sounds like Zac's up."

"Yes, I'm really going to miss him when he's gone. It's been lovely to have young people around."

Lottie smiled. "I'm sure he'll be back the first opportunity that arises. He gets on well with the youngsters here, especially Emma and hopefully next time his two sisters will come with him, not to mention Bill and Sandra."

"Hmm, be a bit like the chocolate box holiday we had at Sea View Cottage." Hetty forced a smile, "What a crazy three weeks that was."

Hetty and Lottie were both in the kitchen making a few bits and pieces for Zac's farewell and pond-warming party that afternoon and although both were feeling a little dejected they were determined that Zac's last day would be one to remember.

"Do you really think that was the knife used to take poor David's life?" Lottie asked as she glanced at the rusty knife lying on the kitchen window sill which Mark had dug up in the garden.

"We'll never know for sure but I wouldn't be surprised. I mean, you could hardly lose something that size when cutting cauli or whatever so I reckon it was buried deliberately."

Lottie nodded. "Probably by George. I mean, I hardly think he'd ever want to see it again after what Polly had used it for."

"If she had."

"Yes, if she had."

Lottie sighed. "This poor house has seen some horrific happenings, hasn't it? I mean, not many houses have witnessed two murders, not linked of course and with seventy plus years between them."

"Three," corrected Hetty, "you mustn't forget Simon's mother, Betty. She died here too and it was no accident."

As Hetty bent down to put a quiche in the oven, the phone rang.

"I'll get it," Lottie wiped her hands, "At least I know it won't be Grace larking around."

As she piled dirty dishes by the sink, Hetty could hear Lottie chatting and she figured it wasn't anyone they knew because her sister's voice sounded formal.

"That was Graham from the art gallery," smiled Lottie, as she returned to the kitchen, "he said he'd like to call tomorrow if that's okay. I said yes but to make it in the afternoon because we have to take Zac to the station in the morning. So he'll be here some time between two and half past."

"Wonderful," cried Hetty, "I'm longing to know if Old Jimmy is genuine. Not that it'll make any difference as he'll always have a place on my wall."

The sun shone brightly all afternoon on the thirty guests who attended the pond-warming farewell party, and to Hetty and Lottie's surprise and delight, several people brought gifts for the sisters; flowers, chocolates, bottles of wine and from Chloe and Colin who ran the guest house next door they received a large realistic looking heron.

"Now all we need are some fish," laughed Lottie, as she stood the heron beside the pond.

"We've already thought of that," said Kitty, as she arrived with Tommy each carrying fish in polythene bags of water.

"Snap," giggled Natalie Burleigh, who carried a similar bag.

"Oh thank you but you shouldn't have," muttered Hetty, as she took the bag from Natalie and Lottie took the bags from Kitty and Tommy.

Hetty squeezed Natalie's hand, "I'm really glad you've come." She turned to Luke, "You too Luke."

To Hetty's surprise Luke kissed her on the cheek. "I've never been one to bear a grudge," He laughed, "anyway, I wanted to see your pond as we intend to have one when we get our house."

"Any luck yet?"

Luke crossed his fingers. "One of the little cottages down in the village along the main street has just come up for sale. We've seen it, we like it and we've put in an offer. Now we're waiting to see if it's accepted."

"Well, I hope it is. I really, really hope it is." Hetty spoke with sincerity.

A familiar voice caused her to turn round. Sid had arrived carrying a lovely white iris. "This is to go in the pond," he chuckled, "and I'm hoping Hetty will be slipping into her bikini when she puts it in the water."

"Cheeky," laughed Hetty, taking the plant from Sid, "but fortunately that won't be necessary as irises prefer shallow water and so it'll go on the marginal shelf. Anyway, how do you know I put my swimsuit on to put the waterlily in the pond?"

Sid laughed. "Grace told me." He bit his lip, "Whoops, I shouldn't have mentioned her, should I? I suppose she's persona non grata."

Hetty squeezed his hands but couldn't find the right words to reply.

Everyone gathered around the pond as the fish were released into the water and several sat mesmerised as they tried to spot the fish as they settled into their new home; Albert shared in the fun, wagging his tail excitedly.

Hetty and Lottie's neighbours along Blackberry Way had loaned them garden furniture for the day and so there were plenty of places to sit and blankets on the grass for those who preferred to lie down.

Zac and Emma who had worked all morning getting the garden ready for the celebration, were glad to take their ease and sit on the lawn with Kyle and his girlfriend, Suzie.

"I didn't know Kyle had a girlfriend," Lottie said to Zac, when they stood side by side at the table beneath a pop-up gazebo helping themselves to food and drinks later in the afternoon.

"No, I suppose we've not mentioned her because she's been away and only came home a couple of days ago. She's been away on a gap year."

"What, for a whole year?"

"Near enough. She went at the end of September last year."

"Goodness me, I know youngsters do things like that these days but I should hate to have been away from family and friends for that long when I was young and I'd like it even less now. Kyle must have missed her dreadfully."

"Well no not really. They'd only been an item for a couple of weeks when she went. Although I think he's known her for some time."

"So has she been anywhere nice?"

"Australia. Apparently she's brilliant at surfing now and is going to teach Kyle and Emma."

"Lovely, and so did she go with friends?"

"No, she went all on her own, back packing and had a brilliant time."

A look of horror crossed Lottie's face. "She must be one very brave young lady. It gives me the shudders just thinking about it."

Much to the delight of Hetty and Lottie everyone present made favourable comments about the pond, the colourful flowers in the back garden, the food and drink on offer and the choice of music.

"I find the pond compliments hard to swallow," sighed Hetty, when she went into the kitchen to fetch more food and saw Lottie slicing up pizzas she had just taken from the oven, "I mean, it wasn't just the work of you, me and Zac, was it? Much of the credit should go to Grace. I wish she could hear what people are saying but sadly under the circumstances, she can't and she never will." Hetty's bottom lip quivered.

Lottie squeezed her sister's hand. "I feel the same way, Het and I'm sure we'll always think of it as Grace's pond."

Inside her Tuzzy-Muzzy room, Grace Dunkerley sat on the broad sill of the open window with her head leaned back against the white wall. From the garden next door she could hear voices chattering and the sound of happy laughter. Music played in the background and through the trees she caught the occasional glimpse of people milling around the pond and strolling along the garden paths.

"I should be there," she whispered, as a tear trickled down her cheek. "And I would be were it not for my brooch." She tried to laugh but the attempt was no more than a squeak. She looked to the sky. "Why did you do it, Mum? This is all your fault and I'm left to pick up the pieces. Simon hates me because you killed his mother. Hetty and Lottie hate me because they think I tried to kill them even though it was not my intent. The only good to have come from this is the knowledge that poor David will eventually be laid to rest with his brother in a proper and respectable manner."

As she leaned forwards the sun caught the blue stones in her brooch. Grace unclipped it and held it in her hand. "And as for you it seems there is a lot of truth in dragonfly folklore." She looked towards the back garden of Primrose Cottage where a glimpse of the pond's water was just visible through the branches of a tree. "If a dragonfly suddenly appears in your life," she whispered, "it means you need to take care because something is hidden or the truth is being kept from you." She laughed scornfully, "The truth was certainly kept from me until earlier this year and now everything I've ever held dear is gone."

She pinned the brooch back onto her collar. "And what I fear most is that I may have inherited the reckless gene that caused my mother to behave so badly." With a heavy heart she stood up. "There's only one thing to do." She then picked up her handbag and left the room.

Zac woke the following morning, looked from the window and saw there was a misty haze hanging over the back garden and the field beyond was completely hidden from view. Feeling sad that the sun wasn't shining for his last morning, he slipped out of bed and went to the bathroom for a shower.

In the kitchen his grandmother was taking a cherry cake that she had made especially for her son, Bill, from the oven so that Zac could take it home with him; his aunt was washing up glasses and dishes from the previous day.

"Just as well the garden party was yesterday and not today," Zac said, trying to sound cheerful.

Hetty nodded. "Your grandmother and I said exactly that ourselves."

"Are you all packed?" Lottie asked, as she picked up a tea towel to dry the dishes.

"Near enough. I did most of it yesterday."

Lottie placed plates she had dried back in the cupboard. "And have you enjoyed your stay with us?"

"It's been the best," said Zac, as he sat down on the stool, "and it's going to feel strange waking up at home in my own bed tomorrow. I'm so glad you asked me. I'll have so much to tell everyone when I get home."

Later in the morning, Hetty and Lottie drove Zac to Penzance station and Emma went along too. They all walked with him down the platform and watched as he boarded the train and put his luggage on the rack above his reserved seat. He then leaned from the window to say his goodbyes and chat until the guard blew his whistle and the train slowly pulled out of the station. Emma walked along with the train until she reached the end of the platform and then she waved until the train was out of sight; when she turned round the sisters saw that she was crying.

Meanwhile, inside Tuzzy-Muzzy, Chloe was busy upstairs doing the guest' rooms. The last one on the landing was Grace's; when she knocked on the door to make sure no-one was in, there was no reply. She unlocked the door and slipped inside; clean towels in one hand, a vacuum cleaner in the other. To her surprise she saw that Grace was in the room and asleep in bed.

"Oh, I'm so sorry," she whispered, "I naturally assumed you were out."

Hastily she turned and retreated towards the door but as she reached for the handle something caused her to pause. She put down the vacuum cleaner and stood perfectly still. The room felt chilly, calm and eerie. There was no sound of breathing. There was no sound at all. Quietly Chloe turned, she tossed the towels onto a chair and crossed towards the bed. An empty gin bottle stood on the bedside cabinet along with an empty pill bottle. Chloe placed her hand on Grace's forehead. It was cold. She attempted to find a pulse. There was none but in her hands Grace held two envelopes. One was addressed to Hetty and Lottie; the other to John Whittingham.

Chapter Twenty-Five

On Monday afternoon, Hetty and Lottie, both shocked and saddened by the death of Grace, pulled themselves together and put on brave faces ready for the visit of Graham from the art gallery. Before he arrived, Hetty took the painting of Old Jimmy downstairs and placed it on the sideboard in the sitting room ready for Graham's inspection. At five minutes past two they heard his car pull up outside their house.

"Would you like a cup of tea?" Lottie asked, as he stepped into the hallway.

"That's very kind but no thank you. I've only just had lunch."

"Please excuse the smoky smell," begged Hetty, observing his nose twitch as he looked around at the cracked plaster on the walls and ceiling and the bare floorboards blackened and scorched, "we had a little fire in here a couple of days ago and the hallway bore the brunt of it."

Graham's eyebrows rose. "I hope the painting wasn't damaged."

"No, no, it's fine. It was safely tucked away on the wall in my bedroom."

They led Graham into the sitting room and offered him a seat near to the window where he would benefit from the natural light. He took a magnifying glass from his briefcase as Hetty handed him the painting. She felt a pang of satisfaction when she saw the expression on his face; he smiled broadly and his eyes sparkled with delight.

After what seemed like an eternity he spoke: "This is indeed the missing picture of Old Jimmy."

"I'm so glad," smiled Hetty, "not that it really makes any difference to me. Old Jimmy has a place on my wall whether he's genuine or not."

Lottie sat down on the settee. "So can you tell us anything about Old Jimmy? I mean, was he a real person or just a made up figure?"

"Oh he was a real person alright." He leaned forward and took a sheet of paper from his briefcase. "I have a few facts and details of him here. Shall I read them to you?"

Hetty clasped her hands. "Oh, yes please."

"Right. Old Jimmy was born in 1862 into a family who were quite affluent and owned several properties in West Cornwall. Nevertheless, Jimmy loved the sea and so he became a dedicated fisherman. In 1884 he joined the Pentrillick Lifeboat crew and ten years later he was made coxswain."

Hetty gasped. "He was on the lifeboat here in Pentrillick? I've gone all goosepimply."

Graham actually laughed. "Yes, and I must admit I think it's amazing that the painting is back in the village he loved so dearly."

"So whereabouts did he live?" Lottie asked.

Graham looked up from the sheet of paper. "Sadly, I can't answer that because there's no mention of it here. It just says he lived in the village."

"Oh, what a shame. Anyway, please continue."

"During the First World War many young men, enticed by Lord Kitchener's famous 'Your Country Needs You' campaign, went to war leaving the lifeboat without some of its most agile young men. And so to help swell the numbers, Jimmy's son who was not a fisherman and cared little for the sea joined the crew."

Hetty raised her hand. "Sorry to interrupt, but didn't they have conscription in World War One then?"

"It's funny you should ask that," said Graham, "because I thought the same thing so looked it up before I came here. Apparently conscription was first introduced in January 1916 for single men aged between eighteen and forty one."

Hetty nodded. "I see and I promise not to interrupt again."

Graham smiled. "I don't really mind if you do." He picked up the sheet of paper and continued to read. "In December 1915 while Jimmy was in bed suffering from a severe bout of flu and delirium, the coastguard observed a fishing boat in distress; it was listing badly and appeared to be drifting towards the rocks. The lifeboat was prepared for launch and the crew prepared to go to sea but Jimmy wasn't to be amongst them; he was deemed too ill. It was a particularly inhospitable afternoon; the wind at the beginning of the day had been fresh but as the day wore on it increased rapidly and by dusk was blowing south westerly gale force eight, gusting storm force ten. Nevertheless, the lifeboat managed to reach the stricken vessel and take off the five-man crew." Graham looked up, "Of course you realise that the lifeboat back then wouldn't have been equipped as they are today. They didn't even have engines and so the crew had to face the elements using oars."

"No, I suppose not," agreed Hetty, "It's easy to forget little things like that."

"And likewise the fishing boat would have been without an engine too and ran, I assume, by sail," added Lottie.

"Correct."

"So did the lifeboat get back okay?" Hetty asked.

Graham nodded. "Yes, but sadly as it began its return journey a fearsome wave tipped the boat and one its crewmen fell overboard and into the sea. The rest of the crew tried hard to rescue him but it was all in vain. The young man drowned. He was Old Jimmy's son and his body was washed up on the beach two days later. Needless to say Jimmy was heartbroken and many thought he'd never set foot on the lifeboat again, but he did. There was after all a war on; he was needed and determined to play his part." Graham's voice croaked with emotion. "Jimmy continued to serve with the lifeboat until the war ended in 1918 and finally stepped down after thirty four years of service. A few years later Pentrillick had a new lifeboat and they called it Old Jimmy after him. He died in 1925 and Choak painted his portrait in 1919."

Lottie was too upset to speak.

"So let me get this right," whispered Hetty, "The Old Jimmy lifeboat was actually named after the Old Jimmy in the picture?"

"Yes, it was."

"Good heavens, it means more to me than ever now. Poor, poor Jimmy. How cruel to have lost his son. It must have wounded him deeply knowing he wasn't there that night to try and rescue him."

Graham nodded. "Yes, I'm sure it did."

Lottie looked at her sister. "I was just thinking, Het, you know when Simon finally remembered the name of Jacob Wheatley he thought he might have drowned in circumstances just as described by Graham. So might Jacob have been Old Jimmy's son?"

Hetty half-smiled. "No, wrong war, Lottie. Old Jimmy's son died in the First World War whereas Jacob Wheatley was on the lifeboat in World War Two. Besides we know Jacob lived 'til he was ninety two because Maisie and Daisy told us."

"Yes, of course silly me. I do get so muddled."

"So, Graham, out of curiosity, do you know the name of Old Jimmy's son?" Hetty asked, "I mean, if Jimmy lived here then it's possible his son might have lived here too."

"Yes, Jimmy's son did live in the village. He and his wife Florence ran the Pentrillick Hotel. His name was Frank, Frank Tregear."

Lottie gasped as her hand flew to her mouth.

Hetty jumped from her chair and looked down on her painting. Her hands were trembling. "So if Old Jimmy was Frank Tregear's father, then he would have been grandfather to David and Peter."

"David and Peter," repeated Graham, clearly confused.

Hetty nodded. "Yes, David and Peter Tregear were twin brothers who sadly both died in 1942."

"I see...I think."

"I wonder," said Lottie, "what Jimmy's proper name was."

Graham looked at it sheet of paper. "James Francis Tregear," he read, "but from the day he was born everyone called him Jimmy."

Three days later, Hetty, Lottie, Tommy and Kitty, Alex and Ginny, walked together into the village to the church where twin brothers Peter and David Tregear were laid to rest together in the grave that had for many years hidden the truth of David's unlawful demise. This time, however, David was buried with dignity and with flowers to show that he was not forgotten even though he had never known those who attended his funeral. And to mark his resting place, Simon Berryman vowed the upturned headstone currently lying by the grave and inscribed only with details of Peter would be professionally cleaned and then David's name added to say the twin brothers were reunited.

Because the mystery of David Tregear's disappearance had captured the imagination of Pentrillick's residents, the funeral was very well attended and so after the interment, it was a large gathering that went to the Crown and Anchor where Simon had arranged for refreshments to be served. Hetty and Lottie proposed to be amongst them but before they left the churchyard Lottie took Hetty by the arm. "Come with me, Het. There's something I need to find and it's probably very near here." She cast her eyes along the headstones in the row where the Tregear brothers lay and moved to the next row.

"Here it is," she said pointing to a large marble headstone. Hetty sighed, "Of course, how silly of us not to have looked before."

Lottie leaned forwards and then read: *In loving memory of Jacob Wheatley. June 27th 1910 - February 21st 2002. Loving husband of Emily and father to Stephen and Rebecca. RIP."*

"Oh dear, it makes me shudder to think of the dreadful accusations we made against poor Jacob when in reality he was a humble farm worker and a loving husband and father," said Hetty, "I feel so guilty. I hope he doesn't know. Wherever he might be." She looked to the sky.

Lottie took her sister's arm. "Well if he does know I'm sure he'll understand and probably even be pleased that the mystery is solved at last. After all we know he was around back then and so he must have been as mystified as everyone else as to where David had gone. Come on, after all this I think I need a very large glass of wine."

"No, no just a minute there's someone else we must find," said Hetty, as she slowly walked along the row reading the headstones. When she stopped she pointed. "Here he is."

Lottie walked to her sister's side and looked at the headstone in front of her. *"In Loving Memory of James Francis Tregear (Jimmy),"* she read, *"1862 – 1925. Lifeboat coxswain. Oh, hear us when we cry to Thee, For those in peril on the sea. RIP"*

"How did we not see this before?" Lottie asked.

"Because we weren't looking in this era, were we?" replied Hetty, "We were looking for Tregears post 1942. I'm so glad we've found him."

"Me too, and on reflection I can see now why Peter didn't join the lifeboat crew. His fear of water must have been caused by the fact his father had drowned when he was just a little boy of three."

"Yes, that must have affected the lad very badly."

"Yet, David became a fisherman and joined the lifeboat."

"Probably because it was in his blood," smiled Hetty, "after all David was Old Jimmy's grandson."

"So was Peter but he was probably more like his mother's side of the family. Just shows that even twins can be very different."

Hetty laughed. "And don't we know it." She took Lottie's arm, "Come on, I think I need a large glass of wine too."

As they stepped back onto the path and followed it around the graveyard towards the gate, they saw Vicar Sam leaving the church.

"Good afternoon, Mrs Burton and Miss Tonkins. I believe you two ladies were very much involved in the search to find our dear friend David."

Hetty looked heavenwards and then smiled sweetly. "Yes, we were but please, please, please call me Hetty. Being addressed as Miss Tonkins makes me feel really ancient."

Lottie nodded. "Yes, and I'm Lottie."

Vicar Sam smiled broadly and linked his arms through those of the sisters. "Hetty and Lottie, please allow me to escort you girls to the pub," He laughed, "Lots of people have told me I ought to get to know you but I've always been cautious just in case you prefer a vicar to be, well, you know, more conventional."

Hetty giggled. "We don't do conventional, do we, Lottie?"

"No, we most certainly do not."

"And what's more," laughed Lottie, "we never drink tea from bone china teacups."

In the Crown and Anchor, Vicar Sam insisted on buying Hetty and Lottie each a large glass of wine and they told him of how the search for David had panned out. He listened intently until he was dragged away by some youngsters who wanted him to play pool.

As Hetty and Lottie walked through the pub in search of their friends, it became obvious that most of the conversations around them were about the events which had taken place in 1942, although everyone it appeared was trying to be subtle and kept their voices low in case Simon Berryman was within earshot. For no-one wanted to upset further a likable man who they all deemed had suffered much since the David Tregear mystery had been resolved. For not only had Simon had to come to terms with the fact his beloved father had been an accessory to murder and helped prevent the lawful burial of his stepbrother, he had also learned that his mother's death was not an accident.

"I wonder why George left the suitcase in the attic when he and Simon moved out in the nineteen sixties," mused Hetty, "I mean surely he must have realised that it might be discovered one day."

"Who knows," sighed Lottie, "Perhaps he just couldn't bear the thought of seeing it again and have all the memories come flooding back. Sometimes things are best left alone. And to be fair were it not for Grace and her antics and the brooch we'd never have got to the bottom of the mystery ourselves, would we? And I suppose George might have realised there was very little in the suitcase to reveal why it was hidden there."

"Yes, I suppose you're right."

Seeing Simon sitting quietly on the terrace where Sheila held his hand, Hetty and Lottie went out to join them.

"We have something for you, Simon," whispered Hetty. She opened up her handbag and withdrew a small item wrapped in tissue paper. "Hold out your hand."

On Simon's palm Hetty placed Grace's blue dragonfly brooch.

"In a note that Grace left for us she asked that we give this to you," said Hetty, "Ethel Berryman to whom the brooch was originally given was after all grandmother to you both. She asked that we tell you she begs your forgiveness. She wanted to write to you in person but couldn't find the right words. She said she is ashamed and apologised profusely to us all."

Simon looked at the brooch. "I can't take it," he whispered. "Please you have it. I feel it belongs in your house along with the ghosts of Berrymans of yesteryear."

"But wouldn't you like it, Sheila?"

Sheila shook her head. "I don't think it would be right, especially if it's likely to upset Simon. Besides, we have no daughters to pass it on to."

"Are you sure?"

Simon nodded. "Yes, I'm very sure and as for forgiving Grace, there's nothing to forgive. She was not the one who murdered my mother and my step-uncle. If the truth be known I feel dreadfully sorry for her," he half-smiled, "even if she did make me ill for a while. She is, was, after all my cousin and I wish she was still alive."

"Of course," mumbled Lottie, "it hadn't jelled with me that you were cousins. How silly…how sad."

Hetty wrapped the brooch back in the tissue paper and dropped it into her handbag. "And looking back I realise it must have been Grace who put the flowers on Peter's grave before he was exhumed. And no doubt the flowers were not just for Peter but for David too."

"Poor Grace. I suppose leaving flowers was as near as she could get to saying she was sorry for what her mother had done." Lottie sighed, "The sins of the fathers shall be visited upon the sons. Such an unfair quote."

Hetty sat down next to Sheila. "You know, I think if I'd been in the same position as Grace then I might have done something similar."

"You mean the flowers?" Lottie asked.

Hetty shook her head. "No, I mean everything."

"Oh, Het, surely you wouldn't have."

"Well, I'd have tried to put people off somehow but I certainly wouldn't have used poison, tampered with car brakes or made a letter bomb because I don't have the knowhow. Whereas Grace, I'm told was a pharmacist prior to her retirement which she took early to nurse her mother."

"Is that right?" Sheila asked, "Little wonder then that she had knowledge of poisons and so forth."

"And everything she did, she did to protect the reputation of her partner," sighed Lottie. "Silly Grace. I'm sure he would have understood."

The following afternoon, Grace's partner, John Whittingham, called at Primrose Cottage to meet Hetty and Lottie, prior to overseeing Grace's body being returned up-country where after her cremation he planned to have her ashes scattered in the village in Derbyshire where she had grown up. He told the sisters that he had briefly contemplated having her ashes scattered in Cornwall near to her ancestors but decided under the circumstances that that was a very bad idea. He also wanted to pass on a cheque to the sisters to pay for damage caused by the fire. He told them that Grace thought if she were to have written them a cheque herself they might have rejected it, whereas if it came from him they'd be more likely to accept it as he could explain the depth of her remorse. This request she made of John in her very last letter written shortly before she took her life.

When he was gone, Hetty and Lottie, touched by the affection John clearly had for Grace, went out into the back garden and sat beside the pond. The early September evening was warm and towards the west a spectacular sunset dominated the sky for as far as the eye could see.

"The nights are really drawing in now, aren't they?" Hetty said.

"Yes, and before we know it the Christmas Wonderland will be up and running again and we'll have been here for a whole year."

"And what a year it's been."

"What was it that Grace told us on the day we put the plants in the pond? About dragonflies, I mean." Lottie asked.

"If a dragonfly lands on you it is seen to be good luck," said Hetty, "and, oh yes, I remember, if you see a dragonfly in your dreams or one suddenly appears in your life, that means that you need to take care because something in your life is hidden, or the truth is being kept from you. Something like that."

"Yes, that's what I thought," sighed Lottie, "and it's true, isn't it? Because Grace *was* keeping something from us."

"But we haven't seen a dragonfly yet," reasoned Hetty.

"Not a real one, no, but don't forget Grace's brooch."

"How could I ever forget Grace's brooch?"

"You know what I mean."

"Yes."

Lottie turned her head and when she saw movement from the corner of her eye, she instinctively glanced down to the pond. When she realised what the movement was, she gasped and shook Hetty by the arm. "Look, Het," she whispered, "Look at the waterlily."

Hetty blinked in surprise for on the waterlily a beautiful blue dragonfly rested on the largest leaf.

"What! A dragonfly…at night…surely not. I mean…."

As her voice faded the dragonfly rose and swooped majestically over each of the new pond's plants. It then drifted upwards above the glistening water, its colours radiant in a fading beam of sunlight. With a swish and a swoop it then flew down and settled in turn on the arm of each sister. Neither spoke as it then rose, flapped its delicate wings and flew off into the sunset.

THE END

Printed in Great Britain
by Amazon